KIDDING!

Andy Griffiths lives in a treehouse with his friend Terry and together they make funny books, just like the one you're holding in your hands right now. Andy writes the words and Terry draws the pictures. If you'd like to know more, read this book (or visit www.andygriffiths.com.au).

Terry Denton lives in a treehouse with his friend Andy and together they make funny books, just like the one you're holding in your hands right now. Terry draws the pictures and Andy writes the words. If you'd like to know more, read this book (or visit www.terrydenton.com).

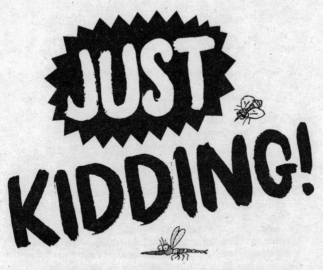

JUST KIDDING!

ANDY GRIFFITHS
& TERRY DENTON

MACMILLAN CHILDREN'S BOOKS

First published 1997 in Mammoth by Reed Books Australia as *Just Tricking*

Pan edition first published 1999 by Pan Macmillan Australia Pty Ltd

This UK edition published 2019 by Macmillan Children's Books
an imprint of Pan Macmillan
20 New Wharf Road, London N1 9RR
Associated companies throughout the world
www.panmacmillan.com

ISBN 978-1-5290-2296-4

1 3 5 7 9 8 6 4 2

A CIP catalogue record for this book is available from the British Library.

Printed and bound by CPI Group (UK) Ltd, Croydon CR0 4YY

CONTENTS

GREAT
FRESHWATER
FISH of the
WORLD #47

The
Thompson's
Gazelle.

... this page
is blank.

This should not be here!!

PLAYING DEAD

t's 8.15 a.m. and I'm still in bed. I should have got up an hour ago.

But I didn't. You want to know why? Because I'm dead.

Well, not really dead. I'm just pretending I'm dead so I don't have to go to school.

This is the start of the first story. We don't need any drawings here...

If I can convince Mum and Dad that I'm dead, not only will I have pulled off one of the greatest practical jokes of the century, but I'll get off going to school for the rest of the year. Maybe even for the rest of my life.

I got the idea from my dog. I've been taking Sooty to obedience classes each Sunday morning. We've only been going for a few weeks, but already he's learned to sit,

or here.

..or here.

That's our son. When he died we couldn't bear to part with him. So we had him stuffed & turned into a lamp.

beg *and* roll over. Yesterday he learned how to play dead. I thought, if my dog is smart enough to do it, then why not me?

All I've got to do is lie here without breathing or blinking. Well, when I say without blinking, I mean blinking when nobody is looking.

And when I say without breathing, I don't mean not breathing at all – that would be stupid. I mean just taking a tiny little breath every so often – just enough to keep me alive.

The only thing that worries me is, I'm such an excellent practical joker, I might trick myself into thinking I'm really dead. And if that happened, I'd be as good as dead – or as bad as dead – because as far as I can see, there's nothing really good about being dead, except that you don't have to go to school.

Suddenly Mum bustles into the room.

'What? Still in bed? Come on, you'll be late!'

I hear the rattle of the curtains being opened.

Hello, I'm a pirahna

2

DO NOT LIFT THE CORNER OF THIS BOOK OR YOU WILL GET A FRIGHT.

The sudden light hurts my eyes, but I remember not to blink.

Any moment now Mum is going to see me. And scream.

She's standing right next to me.

'Pooh, what a stink! When's the last time you cleaned this room? It's an absolute pigsty! Dirty socks and undies everywhere. Why can't you just put them in the washing basket? If you're not showered, dressed and out of this house in ten minutes you're going to be late, and I'm not going to drive you.'

She walks out of the room.

I stare at the ceiling. What else would a real corpse do? It's not as if it would make some brilliantly witty comeback, like, 'I'm not going to school today because I'm dead. Just leave me alone so I can rot in peace.' Yeah – that would be a good line, but I can't say it because I'm supposed to be dead. So, I just lie here and stare at the ceiling some more.

Next thing I know, Dad is standing next to the bed.

'Andy?' he says.

Next time your parents take you to a fancy expensive restaurant, have an eating race with your brothers/ sisters. If the race is close try stuffing food in your ears, up your nose, down your shirt, in the flower bowl or in your shoes.

JUST KIDDING!

I'm sorry... the editor says that piranha should be spelled PIRANHA. Excuse me!!

I don't answer.

'Are you all right?' he says in a slightly deeper voice.

I'm holding my breath. My body is tight.

He puts his hand on my shoulder and shakes me roughly.

'Andy!' he says. 'Andy, I'm warning you . . . if this is another one of your practical jokes, it's not funny! You hear me? Not funny!'

I tense as hard as I can while Dad shakes me. Then he stops and puts his thumb and forefingers around my wrist. He's trying to find my pulse.

Darn! It's the one thing I can't fake. All the same, I try to concentrate on my heart and slow it down.

I read somewhere about these people who use the power of the mind to slow down their heartbeat, so I figure I might as well give it a try.

I imagine that my heart is as still as a rock.

A red rock.

A paralysed red rock.

A frozen paralysed red rock.

What is the next word in this series?

- FOOT
- LEG
- BACK
- NECK
- . . . .

Ans: Pg 24

APRIL 1ˢᵗ should be WORLD PRACTICAL JOKING DAY

Try filling your parents' good work shoes/boots with warm custard. When they slip them on, say: "Happy World Practical etc Day"! They'll love you for it.

I guess that makes me a dumb piranha.

A frozen paralysed red rock in a deep deep sleep.

It seems like forever, but eventually Dad puts my arm back down onto the bed. Gently.

And he says in a quiet voice: 'Andy – now listen to me. You're cold and you're not breathing. You're staring at the ceiling and I can't find a pulse. You may be dead for all I know. But then your past record leaves me no choice but to wonder if this isn't just another one of your so-called "jokes". If you are just kidding around, then I'll give you to the count of three to get out of bed and we'll say no more about it. But, if you don't get out of bed, and I find out later that you're not really dead . . . well . . . you'll wish that you had been. Is that clear?'

He's trying to trick me. He wants me to nod. But I'm not going to fall for it. There's only room for one practical joker around here – and it's not Dad. He starts counting.

DARE YOU
TO STICK
YOUR
TONGUE
IN THE
END OF
AN
ESCALATOR.

'One . . . '

I'm not sure I believe that I won't get into trouble if I confess. He sounds pretty

so, why am I here?

serious. I'll probably end up being grounded for a week. And I'll *definitely* end up having to go to school.

'Two . . .'

What have I got to lose? And, anyway, I've come too far to chicken out now.

'Three!'

I don't move a single muscle.

Dad calls Mum into the room.

'Is everything all right?' she asks.

'I'm afraid I've got some bad news,' says Dad. 'I don't know how, or why, but it appears that Andy is no longer living . . . that is to say, he is . . . er . . . dead.'

'Oh no,' she says, and starts to cry. 'Oh no!'

Out of the corner of my eye, I see Dad move to put his arms around her.

While they're distracted, I quickly take a couple of good deep breaths.

'But he was such a nice boy!' Mum wails. 'Such a *good* boy! He had his problems . . . but deep down he didn't mean any harm.'

'No,' says Dad, 'I don't believe he did mean any harm – he just never knew when to stop.'

Next time your friend is bragging, bet him he can't remove the cheeze from a mousetrap with his nose. (Show him photos (faked) of you doing it)

Keep. Hospitzl number close by.

I have to tell you the page number.

Dad's taking the whole thing better than I expected. I mean, he's usually pretty calm and all, but I would have thought, maybe, he might be a bit more upset. After all, I am his only son.

'Oh well,' he says. 'No use standing around here all day. There's work to be done.'

'But surely you're not going to work now!' says Mum.

'Well,' says Dad, 'somebody's got to dig the hole.'

'What hole?'

'We can't just leave his body here.'

'I suppose not,' says Mum. 'Where are you going to dig it?'

Dad hands her his handkerchief.

'I think beneath the lemon tree might be nice – and it'd be good for the lemons.'

'Yes,' says Mum, 'it's been struggling a bit lately.'

'I'll go get the spade and start digging. I'd like to have him in the ground before lunchtime. Before he starts to smell.'

'Okay,' says Mum, wiping her eyes. 'And while you're doing that, I'll put the kettle on.

AMAZING EYE TRICK #1
↓
Stare at this dot
●
■
and this square for 24hrs, with both eyes closed. Which one seems more round? Ans: pg 82

Dare you to drop a Red hot Iron down your pants. IT WON'T HURT.

7 Boredom maximoso.

I think we could both use a good strong cup of tea.'

I can't believe what I'm hearing. Have my parents completely lost their minds? Are they seriously thinking of burying me in the backyard? Aren't there laws against that sort of thing?

Dad leaves the room.

Mum kneels down beside the bed and kisses me on the cheek. She passes her hand over my eyelids, just like they do in the movies. I'm so touched, I almost forget to close them – but I remember just in time.

'I don't care what anyone says,' she whispers. 'You *were* a good boy.'

Mum leaves the room.

I don't dare open my eyes again. I wouldn't want her to come back and catch me with them open. That would really freak her out. And I think she's been freaked out enough for one day.

Maybe I should confess.

But how do I confess without freaking her out even more? After all, if she thinks I'm dead, and then I walk into the kitchen,

THINGS
TO
DO:

Why not try to convince your brother that barbells make great armbands.

FRESHWATER
FISH OF THE
WORLD #75:
Half of
something,
dunno
what!

what do I say? Somehow, I don't think 'Hi, Mum, I'm not really dead, I was just kidding!' would go down all that well.

FRESHWATER
FISH of the
WORLD № 756:

The other
half.

But if I don't confess, I'm going to be buried in a cold muddy hole in my own backyard.

I'll have worms gnawing at my eyeballs for the rest of eternity. That's a pretty high price to pay for a practical joke. Even one as brilliant as this.

The lemon tree is right outside my window. I can hear Dad digging. And whistling.

Whistling?

I die and he whistles? What is he – some kind of monster? Normal people don't whistle when their son dies. Then again, normal people don't bury bodies in the backyard.

To discover
the best
practical
joke ever,
turn to
Pg 130

But as I listen to Dad's whistle, I begin to notice something strange. It's different from his normal one.

It's too loud.

Too cheerful.

And now it becomes clear.

My parents don't think I'm dead – they just want me to think that they *think* I'm

This is page 6 upside down.

dead. All that stuff about being good for the lemons . . . that's not what it's about at all. They're just trying to teach me a lesson.

They want to scare me.

Well, I don't scare easily. And I'm not about to be beaten at my own game by a couple of amateurs.

Is your family COMPUTER KEYBOARD malfunctioning.

HOW TO FIX IT.

☆1. Fill the bath with mud.

☆2. Screw off all bits that will screw off.

☆3. Carefully chuck the keyboard and bits into the bath.

☆4. Stir with a tennis racket.

☆5. Glue all the bits together again with Hobby Glue.

It should now work perfectly.

After a long morning of lying here with my eyes shut, I'm pretty bored.

At last I hear Dad stop digging.

Mum and Dad come into my room. I know what's coming next.

I suck my breath in and try to remain absolutely still. Dad grabs me underneath my arms. Mum lifts me up by the legs. I try to make my head flop around in a convincing corpse-like fashion. They carry me out to the backyard and lay me down beside the lemon tree.

Dad gets down into the hole – which I can see through my slitted eyes is deeper than I expected – puts his hands back under my arms and pulls me down towards him.

Hey, this is dinner.

My legs follow with a thud.

The mud at the bottom of the hole is cold and wet and almost immediately my pyjamas are soaked through. I'm sure Dad is just dying for me to crack and open my eyes so he can say 'Just kidding!'

But I'm not going to give him the pleasure. Not now . . . not ever.

Dad climbs out of the hole. Mum begins reading from a small blue book, her voice low and serious.

' . . . Ashes to ashes . . . Dust to dust . . . '

Dad is standing to attention, shovel by his side.

I'm starting to wonder if this is such a good idea after all. Dad starts filling in the hole. I don't have to wonder any more. Now I know for sure. This is a *terrible* idea.

First I feel dirt hitting my toes. Then my legs. And then my stomach. A big clump lands on my chest and dirt splatters onto my face.

Something's wrong. It's not possible that I'm such a brilliant actor that my parents really think I'm dead . . . is it?

A great thing to do in your holidays (especially if you're bored) is to cram yourself in the bowl of your washing machine, preset the cold cycle, & go to sleep.

Very tasty mosquito!!

No, that's stupid . . . they'll crack . . . any minute now.

Another handful of dirt splashes across my face.

And another.

And now I don't know what to think . . . because I'm almost completely buried and I'm having trouble breathing.

I open my mouth to shout, 'Okay, you win! I was just kidding!' But a big clump of earth lands in my mouth and I can't get the words out.

Why the long face?

It's dark.

It's quiet.

It's cold.

How long have I been here?

Am I dead?

If I am dead, then how come I'm still thinking?

I know one thing for sure. If I ever get out of this – and it's beginning to look like there's not much hope of that – I'm never

I think the black thing just fell off the end of my nose.

HEY YOU, MOUSE! Pull this handle.

going to play another practical joke for as long as I live.

Hang on, I can feel something on my stomach. Urgent jabbing and scratching. The weight of the dirt on my belly is lifting. When the scratching starts on my chest, I realise what it is.

Sooty has come to save me! He's the only one who realises I'm not dead! He must be able to smell me, to sense my warmth.

And as the weight of the dirt lifts, I decide I don't care about playing dead any more. Anything would be better than this. Even school.

I sit up and scream: 'I confess! You win! I was just kidding!'

I wipe the mud out of my eyes and see my parents staring down at me.

They are shocked.

The sight of me rising from the dead has them goggling at me in horror, their mouths frozen open.

Mum starts screaming. Dad is trying to ward me off with his spade, holding it out in front of him, as if it's a cross and I'm some

Before Breakfast Mechanical YOBA Exercise.

☆ Take your little brother's iPad.

☆ Pull it apart with screwdrivers, hammers & forklift trucks.

☆ Put all the bits in a crisp, new paper bag.

☆ Say: "Here, I fixed this for you!"

☆ RUN !!

13 Page 13.

sort of vampire.

'Dad, it's okay!' I reassure him. 'I was playing a dumb joke and I'm sorry!'

But I might just as well be speaking another language.

My words don't seem to be having any impact on him whatsoever. He's still brandishing the spade as he and Mum back slowly away from the hole.

This joke is completely out of control. The only one who's glad to see me is Sooty. He's standing at the top of the hole trying to lick my face. I push him away but he keeps coming back for more, like it's a game. At least somebody round here is acting normal.

NO MORE
HEART
ACHES!

NEW
IMPROVED
MECHO-
HEART

SIMPLY SCREW
INTO CHEST
& PLUG
INTO
LIVER.
IT REALLY
WORKS!

Then, all of a sudden, Dad drops the spade and clutches at his chest with his right hand. He drops to his knees, his mouth still wide open, then falls forward onto his face.

I leap out of the hole and rush to his side. I roll him over and check to see if he's breathing.

Nothing.

I place my hands on his chest and push with all my weight, just like they showed us

in first aid. I push three more times. Then I
pinch his nose and pull his head back. I'm
about to start mouth-to-mouth resuscitation
when Mum screams.

'Get away from him, you . . . you . . .
zombie!'

'I'm not a zombie!' I tell her. 'I'm not dead
– I was just kidding!'

'Don't touch him, you bloodsucking
freak!'

'Mum, I haven't got time to argue! I've got
to do this. It's Dad's only hope.'

I take a deep breath. Mum starts laughing.
Poor Mum. The stress has affected her
brain. And it's all my fault. But I can't help
her until I've saved Dad. First things first.

I take another breath and am about to
put my mouth over Dad's when he starts
spluttering. First a sputter. Then a wheeze.
And then a deep rocking laugh.

Dad opens his eyes. They are wet with
tears.

'Would you mind sharing the joke with
me?' I ask.

'Sure,' says my father, pulling himself

BEAUTY
TIP.

MIX IN
SOME
GLOW
IN THE
DARK
PAINT
WITH
YOUR
SISTER/
BROTHER'S
ACNE
COVER-UP
BEFORE
THEIR
BIG
NIGHT
OUT.

(In the
disco
their
zits
will
glow like
stars).

Page 3942

15

together with great effort. 'We were *just kidding!*'

And then they really start to laugh. And laugh. And laugh.

They're bent over double. Even Sooty is rolling around on his back, wheezing and carrying on.

It takes a few moments for the shock to sink in, but then I realise that my parents have won.

I've been sucked in.

Sucked in, chewed up and spat out.

But then, maybe things aren't as bad as they seem.

Never mind that I'm wet and cold.

Never mind that I'm covered in mud.

Never mind that I'm the victim of a heartless practical joke that had me thinking I had killed my father and driven my mother insane.

No, never mind all this.

At least I got the day off school.

TRICK
YOUR DAD!
Tease his
nose hairs
& wax them
while he
is asleep.
He'll be so
grateful.
↓
Possible
shapes/
styles

Sorry, on that last page N⁰ I made an error of 3927.

GREAT
COCHROACH
HIDING PLACES
Nº 7:
On a piece
of dental
floss.

Cockroach

'**Y**ou know, there's a world of opportunity out there,' says Mr Bainbridge. 'A world full of opportunities, just waiting for a young man like you. Yes, a world of opportunities!'

'Yes, sir.'

I feel like taking the opportunity to tell him to shut up, but I'm much too polite for that. Besides, Mr Bainbridge is Dad's boss.

I'm under strict instructions tonight to just sit quietly, behave myself and not mess up in any way. The worst thing is, Dad has made me promise not to play any practical jokes.

No squirting flowers. No exploding cans

of peanuts. No rubber vomit.

Dad said that if I tried any funny stuff at the dinner table, my pocket-money would be stopped for a month.

I made the promise, but I don't think Dad realises how hard it is for me. See, the thing is, I'm a practical-joke-a-holic. I need to play practical jokes like other people need to breathe air and drink water.

I don't really see what's wrong with a few harmless practical jokes anyway. They help to break the ice. It's not like I've got a lot to say to Mr and Mrs Bainbridge.

And it's not like they've got a lot to say to me either. Well, Mr Bainbridge does, but it's not so much conversation as a *lecture*.

'Too many kids these days,' says Mr Bainbridge, 'expect opportunity to come to them. But it doesn't work that way. Oh no. You've got to go out and grab – grab it by the collar! When I was a young man – '

'Dinner is served!' says Mrs Bainbridge, coming into the room carrying an enormous bowl of salad.

'Thank goodness!' I blurt out, before I

...thank the sharks that last story finished...

18

can stop myself.

'I beg your pardon?' says Mr Bainbridge.

'Um, I just meant, um, let us be thankful for such a lovely meal,' I say quickly.

Mum and Dad are glaring at me.

'Oh,' says Mr Bainbridge, 'that's all right then. For a moment there I thought you were being impatient. That's the other trouble with young people today. They have no patience – '

'Perhaps you'd like to say grace, Andy?' says Mrs Bainbridge. 'The lasagne is getting cold.'

'Oh, ah, yes,' I say.

It's been so long since I said grace, I can barely remember the words.

Everybody closes their eyes.

For a moment I'm tempted to say, 'Two, four, six, eight – bog in, don't wait!' but then I remember Dad's warning.

'For what we are about to receive . . . '

I know I should have my eyes shut too, but somebody's got to keep theirs open to make sure that everyone else's stay closed. And, as I'm the one saying grace, it might as

GREAT
ROACH
HIDING
PLACES
Nº42: on
a tooth
brush,
between
bristles
and
paste.

The
fork!!

19

So far there have been 17 to's, two toos and one two in this story.

Count them!

HA

well be me.

But, as I'm trying to think of the next line, I see something in the salad bowl. Something oval. Something dark brown. Something that looks a lot like a dead cockroach.

At least, I think it's dead. It's sort of hard to tell. All I know is, there's a cockroach in the salad, and it probably wasn't put there on purpose. Unless Mr and Mrs Bainbridge eat cockroaches – which seems unlikely. I mean, Mr Bainbridge must get paid more than Dad, and we don't have to eat cockroaches.

'May we be truly thankful . . .'

Truly thankful? For a *cockroach*?

This would be funny if it wasn't so serious.

I can't just put up my hand and say, 'Excuse me, but there's a dead cockroach in the salad.' It would make it look like the Bainbridges have a really dirty kitchen. They'd get really embarrassed because they'd think that we think that cockroaches fall into their food all the time.

But even worse still, Dad might think that I put it there for a joke. And that would mean trouble.

20

I have to get it out before anybody notices. For everybody's sake.

I grab my spoon to scoop the roach off the salad leaf . . .

GREAT COCKROACH HIDING PLACES Nº 12: Up someone's nose when they first wake up.

'Amen,' says Mr Bainbridge, finishing grace for me as he opens his eyes.

He picks up the salad bowl.

'Salad, Andy?'

'Yes please,' I say. Luck is running my way.

Mr Bainbridge passes me the bowl. I scoop a large portion of salad onto my plate, including the top two pieces of lettuce with the dead roach in between.

Q: Do you know the I.Q. of an average Cockroach?
A: (a) 120 (See pg. 98)
(b) 240 (See pg 122)

So far so good.

Mrs Bainbridge places a large slab of lasagne on the other side of my plate. Normally my mouth would be watering, but the cockroach has kind of taken the edge off my appetite.

'Would you care for some potatoes, Andy?'

Mrs Bainbridge passes me a bowl full of steaming spuds. I pick out one and pass the bowl to Mr Bainbridge.

Now that the roach is on my plate, all I

21

have to do is get it into my pocket before anybody notices.

But first I have to distract them.

'What a beautiful landscape!' I point to a painting on the wall above Mum's head.

Everybody turns to look.

I lift up the piece of lettuce. But the cockroach has other ideas.

It's not dead.

It jumps off the lettuce leaf onto the table and starts running.

Straight towards me.

The roach reaches the edge of the table and tumbles onto my lap. I try to brush it onto the floor, but it disappears underneath my napkin.

Luckily, the others are all still studying the painting. Nobody else has seen the roach's 30-centimetre sprint. I discreetly lift the corner of my napkin to see where the roach has got to, but it's not there. I feel a gentle pricking on my stomach. It's underneath my shirt!

I freeze. The roach crawls around my side and onto my back.

AMAZING EYE TRICK #2:
Stare at these 3 lines

| | |

through a magnifying glass. Which one looks most like the emotion of envy?
Ans Pg 54.

I guess I could crush it by pushing myself back hard against the chair. It would probably work, but I can't bring myself to do it because I can't stand the thought of having squashed cockroach all over my back.

'Are you keen on art, Andy?' asks Mrs Bainbridge.

'I like it,' I say, 'but I'm not very good at it.' I'm trying hard not to panic.

'Ah!' says Mr Bainbridge. 'But practice makes perfect! If a fellow really wants to do something badly enough and he's prepared to apply himself for long enough, then . . . '

'Yes dear,' says Mrs Bainbridge. 'That's all very well, but perhaps Andy doesn't want to be an artist. What are your favourite subjects, Andy?'

I'm trying hard to concentrate on the conversation, but it's not easy. The roach has relocated itself underneath my left arm. I can hardly breathe. It feels like it's burrowing into my armpit.

'I guess I like English the best.' I gasp. 'Not too crazy about maths or science.'

'No, no, no!' says Mr Bainbridge. 'You

SORRY, the best practical joke ever is really on Pg 84

don't want to neglect your maths and science. Keep your options open, that's what I say. Science and technology – that's where the opportunities are.'

Mrs Bainbridge rolls her eyes.

I'd feel sorry for her if I wasn't feeling so sorry for myself. I only have to put up with him for one night. She has to live with him 24/7.

Answer from Pg 4
• FOOT
• LEG
• BACK
• NECK
• DRAJB*

* Ancient Croat word meaning SMELLY PIT DUG IN THE GROUND

The roach has finished playing in my armpit and now I can feel it crawling down my chest.

It's burrowing into my belly button.

I can't stand it any more. I have to get rid of it. I ask for directions to the bathroom and excuse myself from the table.

The bathroom is upstairs. I latch the door behind me and yank off my T-shirt. It flies across the room, skims the top of the toilet bowl, and lands in a heap beside it. But the roach is not on my chest.

Or my back.

Uh-oh – not a moment to lose!

I kick my shoes off, and peel off my trousers and underpants in one swift movement.

flea collar

Well, that was educational.

42, 4, 2. Count them.

24

I'm completely naked – except for my socks – but I still can't find the roach.

There are only two places it can be – one of which is too horrible to even think about.

I study the pile of clothes carefully. The roach emerges from the bottom of my jeans. It's creeping up the left leg. I pick up one of my shoes. Very slowly – so that the roach doesn't notice – and raise it high above my head.

GREAT
C/R
HIDEOUTS
№ 81:
On the
tip of a
lipstick.

The roach reaches the bottom button of my fly.

I take a deep breath.

But something holds me back. If I smash it right there, I'm going to end up with it splattered all over the front of my jeans.

Not a good look.

I put my shoe down slowly. The roach crawls back inside my jeans.

I bet there's a bucket waiting on the other side of this door.

There's got to be a better way than splattering.

I look around for inspiration.

There's a window above the toilet. It's high and very small, but it might do. I could climb up there, hold the jeans outside the window and shake the cockroach off.

No sweat. No splatter. No roach.

I pick up the jeans, taking care to hold the waist and the trouser legs closed so that the roach can't escape. I shut the lid of the toilet and use it to step up onto the cistern. The window is now level with my head.

I lean against the wall for balance and slide the window open as far as it will go. I push the jeans out of the window and shake them as hard as I can.

Suddenly, the roach is on my hand. I get such a fright, I drop the jeans, lose my footing and crash down into the bath.

I feel like lying here, closing my eyes, and pretending it's all just a bad dream – but I have to find the roach before it disappears again. I get out of the bath and study myself in the mirror.

The roach is sitting on top of my head.

This time I know exactly what to do. It's not going to be pleasant, but it's the only way. This is one tricky cockroach and I can't afford to take any chances.

I go back to the toilet and get down onto

my knees. I lift the lid and bend lower and lower until my head is right inside the bowl. Then I take a deep breath, reach up and push the flush button.

It's horrible.

Toilet water up my nose.

Toilet water in my ears.

Toilet water in my mouth.

Finally, the flushing stops. I sit back up.

It's gone.

But so are my jeans.

I can't go back to the table without them. What would I say? I can just imagine the conversation:

MRS BAINBRIDGE: Where are your trousers, Andy?

ME: Oh, I accidentally dropped them out of the bathroom window, Mrs Bainbridge.

MR BAINBRIDGE: That's the trouble with young people today – always dropping their trousers out of bathroom windows, blah blah blah blah blah . . .

Meanwhile, back in the real world, I'm naked from the waist down.

There's no choice, really, but to climb

out the window and fetch my jeans. I can't afford to go a month without pocket-money.

I climb back on top of the cistern and lean across to the tiny window. It's going to be a tight squeeze, but since I haven't eaten any dinner yet, I think I can make it.

I grip the narrow ledge and pull myself up and halfway out.

It's a long way to the ground. I didn't realise I was so high up.

But I'm in no danger of falling.

I'm stuck.

I can't go forward and I can't go back.

And to make matters worse, there's someone banging on the door.

'It's taken!' I yell.

'Is everything all right?' calls Mum. 'You've been in there an awfully long time!'

'Yes,' I call. 'I'll be out in a second.'

'He's not answering!' says Mum. 'I think there's something wrong!'

She can't hear me because my head is outside the house.

Then I hear Mr Bainbridge's voice.

'Stand back, everyone. I'm going to break

60, can you believe that? 5, 3. Wow!

the door down.'

Oh great. My hero.

I hear a huge crash.

Mr Bainbridge is no muscle man, but the flimsy lock snaps like it's made of plastic.

'What the . . . ?' says Mr Bainbridge.

For probably the first time in his life, Mr Bainbridge is speechless, but I guess the last thing he expected to see was my bare bum staring at him from his bathroom window.

'Oh my!' says Mrs Bainbridge.

'Oh no!' says Mum.

'Andy!' says Dad.

'I know this seems a little unusual,' I yell, 'but there's a perfectly reasonable and logical explanation! See, while I was saying grace, I saw this cockroach in the salad bowl, only I didn't want to say anything because . . . '

But I might as well be telling it to the man in the moon.

Mum and Dad and the Bainbridges are too busy going on about ladders and fire brigades and irresponsible young people to listen to my perfectly reasonable and logical explanation.

I close my eyes and wonder if I'll be able to interest anybody in bidding for the TV, magazine, film and book rights to my story, and whether the proceeds will make up for the pocket-money I'm about to lose.

One door closes, another opens.

Like Mr Bainbridge says, there's a world of opportunities out there.

DANGEROUS COCKROACH HIDING PLACES.

1.
Between biscuit + cheese.

2.
Between eyelid & eye.

3.
On the blades of a food processor.

...this story ends here

...go on to next story

68 to's, 6 too's and only a miserly 3 two's. Wow, statistics can be so interesting.

Gorillagram

I have long, shiny black hair and big grey feet with black toe-nails. I have enormous hands with big stubby fingers. I have a spiky black mohawk, a big flat nose and a mouth that moves.

Normally, you would find a creature like me in the jungle or in a zoo, but tonight I am loose on Lygon Street.

I am headed for a restaurant called La Trattoria, where Jen, my sister, is having her sixteenth birthday party.

If you didn't know I was wearing a gorilla suit you would swear that I was a real gorilla. That is, until I start dancing and singing 'Happy Birthday'.

Real gorillas don't sing 'Happy Birthday'. Real gorillas don't sing much at all.

Not the ones I've seen in the zoo, anyway. I guess there's not much to sing about when you're stuck in the same enclosure day after day with all these human beings staring at you.

A GORILLA?
↓

No... Andy

There's not that much to sing about when you're stuck in a gorilla suit, either.

It's a pretty weird experience. You feel sort of cut off from the world. It's like you're there but not there at the same time.

And to make things worse, the suit is about ten sizes too big.

I've only had it on for ten minutes and already I'm boiling hot. I can't see properly because the mask keeps falling forward over my eyes. I have to keep pulling it back against my face, which is a pain, because the inside is already slimy with sweat and stinks of rubber.

Gorilla pretending to be an incinerator. (Tricked me)

Everybody I pass either stares or waves at me. They're all trying to figure out what a gorilla is doing on Lygon Street. To tell you the truth, I'm starting to wonder myself.

32

I'm a new fish.

At last I come to the restaurant, but I can't open the door. My hands are swimming in these big rubber gorilla gloves.

Luckily, one of the waitresses opens it for me. I feel like I should say thank you, but I can't, because real gorillas don't speak English.

The restaurant is full of people. They all turn to look at me.

Jen's party is on the second floor. I pull my mask back tight across my face for the five thousandth time and hunch over to the spiral staircase in the middle of the room. I pass a woman in a purple dress who says to her friends in a know-it-all voice, 'It's just a gorillagram.'

Talk about a party-pooper.

The staircase is difficult to climb because my feet are so large and the steps are so small. When I get to the top, I look across the restaurant at Jen's table. She's sitting with her back to me.

I creep up behind her and put my paws over her eyes.

'Who is it?' she asks.

AMAZING EYE TRICK #1: Stare at this spot for twenty minutes with your left thumb in your right nostril. Now, does this page appear to be 3D. No? It didn't for us, either.!!

A very rare steak, indeed.

The other one was so boring. We had him replaced.

33

I don't say anything.

'Come on,' she says, trying to pull my hands away. 'I give up.'

I crouch down, put my head close to hers and take my hands away.

She screams.

I jump up and start dancing around the table. I can't see properly. The inside of the mask is dripping with perspiration.

All I can taste is rubber.

Mechanical Martini

I knock my knee on a corner of the table. It hurts like hell but I don't stop dancing.

I start singing a version of 'Happy Birthday' without words – just grunts.

Everybody is laughing. Jen's friends, Mum and Dad, the people at the surrounding tables – everybody, that is, except Jen.

'I know it's you, Andy,' she says. 'You're an idiot! Go away!'

When I finish singing, I go up and put my arm around her. I growl really loudly and give her a big sloppy kiss on the cheek.

'Get lost!' she says. 'I mean it!'

But I'm just starting to enjoy myself. I put my hand into her plate of spaghetti and

Do you like my hat?

pretend to scoop it into my mouth, but I deliberately miss and smear it all over my face. Jen is not impressed.

'Get out of my dinner!' she says. 'I can't eat that now. Why do you have to wreck everything?'

She picks up the whole bowl and tips it over my head. Strands of spaghetti and pesto sauce slide down in front of my eyeholes.

But I don't get mad.

I grab a glass of water, drink a big mouthful and, standing on one leg with my arms out to the side – like a fountain – I begin to squirt the water through my teeth. All over Jen. She starts screaming at me.

'Andy – that's enough!'

That's Mum. And she means it.

Time to go.

I put my arms over my head, like I know I've been a very naughty gorilla, and skulk towards the stairs.

I forget that my feet are too big for the steps and end up in a heap at the bottom.

Not a very dignified exit, but definitely a gorillagram they'll never forget.

I pick myself up off the restaurant floor as if nothing out of the ordinary has happened – as if this is the way gorillas always come down stairs.

Some women are watching me and smiling. One of them is the woman in the purple dress.

Just a gorillagram, eh?

A GORILLA?
↓
No, it's Andy again!

I lope up to their table like I'm the sweetest gorilla on earth, just coming up to have my head scratched. Then, without warning, I raise my arms and roar as loudly as I can. They all jump back in fright.

It works better than I'd expected.

In fact, they get such a fright that I get a fright myself. With my heart racing, I make it back out onto the street.

I was going to go back to the car and change, but I'm too pumped up. This suit has powers I never even dreamed of.

You don't want CRAYFISH. No. No. It's not nice this time of year

There is a seafood restaurant next door to La Trattoria. Everybody is staring at me through the window. It's weird. I'm feeling less and less like a human being.

This must be what it feels like to be one

KNOCK KNOCK

That's better.

of the gorillas at the zoo – being stared at all day long. People watching you eat. People watching you go to the toilet. People watching you while you're trying to watch TV.

Except for one important difference – I'm outside on the street, free. The human beings are the ones who are trapped.

I start to imagine that I have just escaped from the zoo, and that I am seeing the street and it's inhabitants for the first time – as if the human world is the zoo and I am the visitor.

New Gorilla head bowling balls.

I move up to the window and press my face against it.

I start staring back at the humans – pointing and poking my finger against the glass.

The humans are not quite sure how to take this. Some smile. Others just stare back blankly. They're not used to being watched.

Who ordered SEA FOOD?!

An old man and lady are sitting at the table nearest the window. They are not taking any notice of me. I ignore the other patrons and study the old couple intently.

They just keep eating and talking, as if I'm not there.

I break off a couple of twigs from a tree on the edge of the footpath and hold one in each hand.

As the old man cuts his food with his knife, I cut an imaginary plate of food with my twig. As he puts the food into his mouth with his fork, I put the imaginary food into my mouth with my other twig.

The man looks at me. He says something to the old lady. She looks at me and waves her hand dismissively.

I ask myself what a real gorilla would do in this situation and the answer comes to me.

I turn around, bend over and moon them. I hoot loudly and run down the street to the next restaurant.

I can't stop laughing.

That old couple will probably spend the rest of their lives wondering why on earth they were mooned by a gorilla.

This is better fun than gorillagrams. I am a gorilla with a get-out-of-zoo-free card

It's like dog poo.

and I'm not going to waste a second.

At the next restaurant I don't press my face against the window. I don't imitate anybody. I just stand gawking.

After a few minutes, one of the waiters comes out. He seems a little nervous.

'Um, er, ah . . . ' he says in a shaky voice. 'Can I help you?'

I cock my head to the side, as if I don't understand.

'Can I help you?' he asks again after a long pause.

I step towards him.

He steps back.

I grunt.

'I'm sorry, sir, but I really must ask you to move away from the window or I will have to call the police.'

I grunt again and step closer to the little man. He stands his ground.

I reach out and give him a big hug.

But he doesn't freak out. He hugs me back. The people inside the restaurant applaud.

I grunt, release the waiter and pat him on the head. Then I give a low bow, turn around and walk on down the street.

I'm having such fun visiting all the restaurants along Lygon Street, that I lose track of the time.

I'm not sure how much later it is when I return to the seafood restaurant. The old man and lady are gone, but a couple of girls are sitting at their table.

I dance around, trying to get their attention.

I'm dancing pretty well I think – for a gorilla – but the girls are not interested. They are looking at something behind me.

That's when I notice the flashing blue light reflecting off the restaurant window.

I turn around. There are two police officers – a man and woman – crouched beside a police car.

Uh-oh.

The man is talking into the handpiece of his radio. The woman is holding a gun. The gun is pointed at me.

Time to become human again.

'Don't shoot!' I yell. 'I'm not a real gorilla! It's just a gorilla suit!'

The policewoman brings her left hand up to her gun so that now she is holding it with both hands.

'Stay there, big fella!' she says. 'Don't move. Everything will be all right.'

'No, you don't understand,' I say. 'You're making a terrible mistake!'

But either she's not listening, or my voice is muffled by the mask, because she keeps that gun pointed right at my chest.

I realise that the quickest way to convince her that I'm not a gorilla would be to take my mask off.

New all electric Gorilla. (very handy)

I grab the hair on top of my mask and pull. But it won't come off.

I can't undo the eyelets that attach the back of the head to the suit because my hands are inside the big rubber gloves. And I can't get the gloves off because I need the use of my fingers to undo the press-studs on the cuff.

'Come on,' I say. 'I know it looks real, but it's just a suit, okay? Just a dumb gorilla suit.'

'Okay, boy,' says the policeman. 'It's okay.

Typical Gorilla paw pvints. (This one's wearing high heels)

Page 41, by the way. And where's my hat?

We don't want to hurt you. Just want to get you back to the zoo where you belong.'

'I don't belong in the zoo!' I yell. 'I'm a human being! I'm wearing a suit, but I can't get it off!'

The police look at each other. They frown.

'What do you think he's trying to say?' says the policewoman.

A GORILLA?

No, it's a dog, Idiot!!

'I don't know, but he sure seems to be trying to tell us something.'

'Almost human, aren't they?'

'Yeah, it's scary.'

'I am human, you idiots!' I bellow.

Then I have a brainwave. I'll sing 'Happy Birthday'. That will prove beyond a doubt that I'm not a gorilla.

I start singing at the top of my voice.

'Why is it making that horrible noise?' says the policewoman.

'I'm not sure,' says the policeman. 'Sounds like it's in pain.'

I hear applause and laughter coming from the other side of the street. A large crowd has formed. And Jen is amongst them! What a relief!

Thank you, dog breath!

42

'Jen!' I call. 'Jen! Help me!'

She doesn't move.

'Jen!'

I jump up and down and point to her.

'That's my sister!' I say to the officers. 'Ask her! She'll tell you I'm not a gorilla!'

But Jen makes no attempt to come across to me. She just stands there scowling, her arms folded.

'Excuse me, young lady,' calls the policewoman. 'This might be a silly question, but do you know this gorilla? It seems to know you.'

Jen looks me up and down.

She hasn't forgiven me for the gorillagram. Or for what I did to her spaghetti.

In fact, it was probably Jen who called the police.

I know she'll help me, but it will take some serious grovelling.

'I'm sorry for the gorillagram, Jen,' I call. 'I didn't mean to wreck your party. I'll make it up to you, I promise. Anything you want. I'll give you money – I'll be your slave for a week – I'll give you all my Easter eggs next

Excuse me, are there any stories about mechanical birds in this book?

No, RACK OFF.

BAD Mr Cockroach

SPLAT!!

happy y!!!

Now I can smell baby poo.

Easter. You name it, it's yours. Can you just tell these police who I am? Come on, Jen, please . . . this is serious!'

But my words are drowned out by the roar of a large green truck with ZOO painted on its side. The truck screeches to a stop behind the police car.

A zoo-keeper armed with a net and a tranquilliser gun jumps out.

'Well?' says the policewoman to Jen.

'Now, Jen, now! Tell her!' I call.

Jen shakes her head.

'Are you kidding?' she says to the police. 'I've never seen that gorilla before in my life.'

The zoo-keeper drops to her knees, takes aim and fires.

I feel the prick of the tranquilliser dart, followed by intense drowsiness.

I slump down onto the footpath.

The zoo-keeper throws the net over me. 'We'll have you back in the zoo in no time.'

'I'm . . . not . . . really . . . a . . . gorilla . . .' I mumble sleepily.

The zoo-keeper pats me gently on the shoulder. 'That's what they all say,' she says.

44

Door-knockers Anonymous

Thursday night.

Mum and Dad have gone out and left me at home all by myself.

Normally I would be making prank phone calls, setting up buckets of water over half-opened doors and putting rubber snakes under pillows – but not tonight.

Tonight I'm standing on a ladder polishing the light bulbs in the lounge with Dad's CD cleaning cloth.

Don't tell me. I know what you're thinking. You're thinking, Andy, if your parents really have gone out and left you all alone, why are you wasting precious practical joke preparation time polishing light bulbs?

Why aren't you making prank phone calls, setting up buckets of water over half-opened doors and putting rubber snakes under pillows?

Well, the reason is that tonight I've decided to clean up the house as a surprise for Mum and Dad. I'll admit, it might seem a bit unusual to polish light bulbs, but the trick to making a place look really clean is in the details. And believe me, I have to make this place look *really* clean.

See, Mum and Dad have gone up to my school for parent-teacher interviews and I already know that my reports are not going to be that great. Lousy, in fact.

A bucket of 3 week old whale vomit, He He

It's not my fault, though. I've worked really hard this year, but my teachers are all against me. They think that just because I spend a lot of time talking and laughing in class, I'm not concentrating. But what they don't realise is, I can't help talking and laughing in class because I get so excited about schoolwork. I've tried to explain this to them, but they won't listen. It's like I said – they're all against me.

New fish. The other one's sick. Must've been something he ate.

So what I've decided to do is tidy up the house and make it absolutely clean and spotless – right down to the very last light bulb. That way, when Mum and Dad come home fuming about my lousy reports and launch into their 'it's time we had a little talk' routine, they're suddenly going to be struck by how beautiful the house is looking and they'll forget all about lecturing me.

They'll be so impressed that I cleaned up the house without being asked that, as a reward, they'll let me eat a whole bucket of chocolate ice-cream and stay up till midnight. It's a lucky thing for me that my parents are so gullible; otherwise I might have been in a lot of trouble.

I'm halfway through polishing the second light bulb on the chandelier. There's a knock on the door. It can't be Mum and Dad because they're not due back for at least half an hour.

I climb down the ladder and open the front door. But there's nobody there.

'Hello!' I call. 'Hello?'

No answer.

That's strange. Whoever it was must be really impatient. I hate that.

I close the door, climb back up the ladder and continue polishing the light bulb.

There's another knock at the door.

'Hang on,' I yell, 'I'll be right there.'

I practically jump off the ladder, and rush to the door.

I open it.

Nobody there.

This is obviously somebody's idea of a joke. And I can guess exactly who that somebody is – Danny Pickett.

Poor Danny. That guy is a compulsive door-knocker. He can't bear to walk past a house without knocking on the front door and running away. I reckon he should join Door-Knockers Anonymous.

He's probably out in the garden somewhere right now, laughing at me.

'Danny!' I call. 'You might as well come out. I know it's you.'

I peer into the darkness but I can't see him anywhere.

'Okay,' I say, 'have it your way.'

Page 49.

One last scan of the garden and I close the door. Let him freeze if he wants.

I've hardly put my foot on the first rung of the ladder when he knocks again. But this time I don't answer it.

He knocks again. And again.

I climb to the top of the ladder and start polishing the third light bulb. I concentrate on it to help block out the sound of the knocking.

Ouch. It hurts my eyes to look at it for so long.

Danny's still knocking, but I'm not going to open the door. It will only encourage him and make me look like an idiot. He can knock until his knuckles are red-raw and he's bleeding to death right on our front doorstep. See if I care.

Yeah, see if I care.

I don't care . . .

Yes I do! I do care!

It's driving me crazy.

He knocks on and on and on. He's not going to stop until I open the door.

I jump off the ladder, sprint to the door

If you desire access to the best practical joke ever be QUICK! Do not delay. TURN TO Pg 9.

C'mon puss. Hungry puss. Eat the nice food.

Page 52.

and open it – all in one fluid movement. I'm going to catch him and kill him. But even before I open the door I know I'm too late.

He's gone. Nobody but the wind. A flurry of brown autumn leaves blows through the door and onto the carpet – the carpet that I vacuumed only fifteen minutes ago. I slam the door.

This means war. I'll be ready for him next time. Danny's fast on his feet, I'll give him that. But when it comes to brain-power, he's no match for me.

I go to the laundry and grab the yellow plastic bucket. I take it back to the kitchen and fill it to about halfway with white flour. I put the bucket on the table and go into the pantry. I take out a bottle of tomato sauce, a bottle of soy sauce, a tin of blackberry jam, a can of tomato paste, a jar of corn relish, a bottle of vinegar, a can of spaghetti, a jar of peanut butter, a jar of Marmite, a dozen eggs, a jar of honey, a packet of cornflakes and a small jar of crushed chilli peppers.

I tip all the ingredients into the bucket and start mixing them up with a wooden spoon. It's hard work because the mixture is so heavy and gluggy.

I add heaps of water and spoon the sludge around and around. That's better. And now I have a whole bucketful of the stuff.

I can't wait to see Danny's expression when, just as he's about to knock, I whip open the door and throw it all in his face. That ought to cure him of door-knocking, once and for all.

-Mouth Open...

C'mon Snore! SNORE!!

After about ten minutes of mixing there's still a lot of lumps, so I get out the blender and pour a litre or so into the jug. I set it to high and flick the switch.

Suddenly, there's reddish-black stink-sauce everywhere. All over me, and all over the kitchen.

I forgot to put the lid on the blender. I hate that.

Once it's all pretty-well mixed, I carry the bucket up the hall to the front door. The bucket's so full and the mixture's so runny that, no matter how slowly I walk, it slops over the sides, all the way up the hall. Never mind – plenty of time to clean that up after

I've dealt with Danny.

I set the bucket down on the carpet and crouch down to wait.

Danny will be back any minute now. I know Danny. He thinks that if something is funny once, then it will be a thousand times funnier if you do it a thousand more times.

I know how he thinks. He'll figure I've left the door by now. But he's wrong – I'm here, waiting.

I'll hear him step onto the porch. I'll hear him open the wire door. And just before he knocks, I'll open the door and give him a bath.

The house is very quiet, except for the sound of tree branches brushing against the roof.

I've got my ear pressed up against the crack of the front door so I can hear even the tiniest movement on the verandah.

I hope he comes soon. The fumes from the sludge are making my eyes water. I need to get a peg to put over my nose, but I don't dare leave the front door. Timing is crucial.

Did you notice my legs?? Cute eh?

A mosquito whines around my head. I grab at it, but I miss and it flies up towards the hall light. I start to get up to have another go at it when I hear a footstep on the verandah. I crouch back down.

More footsteps. He's coming all right.

I move my hand up to the doorknob. I'm so wound up, I'm shaking. I've got to get this exactly right.

I strain to hear him. Another footstep. He must be at the verandah door now. It creaks as he opens it.

I can see him in my mind's eye – in slow motion – pulling the door open. Curling the fingers of his left hand into the knocking position. Drawing his hand back. Stifling a giggle with his other hand as he raises his arm, ready to strike.

That's it. Now!

I open the front door and heave the contents of the bucket onto Danny. It's a perfect throw. I've caught him red-handed. He's covered in the stinking gooey brew. I can't even see his face. Revenge!

He gasps and wipes some of the chunky

stew out of his eyes.

I realise I've made a terrible mistake.

It's not Danny.

'Mum?' I say.

She gasps again.

This is not good. And to make things worse, Dad appears behind her.

'What's going on?' he says, looking at Mum and then at me.

'Um, er . . . ' I say. That's all I can think of. Pretty pathetic really.

The mixture is everywhere. All over the entrance hall, all over the verandah door and all over Mum. She's standing there looking like the creature from the black lagoon. The goo slimes off her clothes and collects in a puddle at her feet.

She is just gasping and shaking her head. Nothing in all her years of putting up with my jokes has prepared her for this.

'I think we need to have a little talk,' says Dad softly. He appears calm, but his ears are very red, and they're trembling – that's not a good sign.

Not that I'm worried.

Any moment now they're going to notice the inside of the house and see how clean it is. Except for the kitchen, of course. And the sludge on the hall carpet and around the entrance. But that's easily fixed. Once they notice the light bulbs they'll calm down.

Any moment now I'll have them eating out of the palm of my hand. Any moment now. It's just a matter of time.

Tragic really

TELL YOUR MUM I SAVED YOU!

i'm standing right on the edge of this huge boulder, looking over Sealers Cove on one side – where we camped last night – and Refuge Cove on the other. There's a cool breeze. I close my eyes and imagine I'm the last person on earth. It's so peaceful. A three-night bushwalk in Wilsons Promontory can be hard work, but it beats school any day.

Suddenly I feel a large hand clamp down on each of my shoulders. I'm shoved forward. My stomach drops. My life starts to flash before my eyes. Then, just as suddenly, the hands pull me back.

'Tell your mum I saved you!'

I turn around. Roseanne O'Reilly is grinning widely.

'You idiot!' I shout. 'What a dumb trick! I could have been killed!'

'It's lucky I was here to save you then,' she says. 'You should be thanking me.'

'Thanks for nothing,' I say.

It's a typical Roseanne joke. Dumb and dangerous. She's been pulling this trick on everybody since we left Tidal River yesterday morning. It's her first time bushwalking. She's new to the school. I don't know why she decided to join the bushwalking club. Probably because no other club would have her.

For advice on how to fix a blister on the toe, turn to pg65

O'Reilly swaggers back to the trail where the rest of the group are resting against their packs.

'You should have seen Andy's face,' she announces to the party. 'He was really scared!'

Not that anybody cares. They're as sick of Roseanne as I am.

Danny comes over.

'Trail mix?' he says.

He hands me a plastic bag full of chocolate

whew... back again... thought I'd got lost.

buds, sultanas, oats, peanuts and sunflower seeds. I take a big handful and pass the bag back. My hands are still shaking from the fright.

'Don't feel bad,' he says. 'Roseanne punched me in the nose this morning.'

'Really?' I say. 'Why?'

'She asked me if I wanted to smell some cheese. Before I could answer, her fist was right in front of my face, and then POW!'

'She didn't wait for your answer? That's not a practical joke – it's just a punch in the face!'

'Tell me about it,' says Danny. 'She made my nose bleed too.'

'What did you do?'

'Nothing. She's bigger than me.'

'Fair point. But we can't let her walk all over us like this. We've got to get her back. Got to teach her a lesson.'

'Sure,' says Danny through a mouthful of trail mix. 'But how?'

I sit on the boulder and use a twig to prise a pebble out of the tread on my boots. Suddenly the answer is clear.

The author recommends to anyone wishing to get more out of this story, the placing of a plastic bucket over your head, while reading!

WOW!?

BUSH TUCKER

One of my legs has been bitten off!!

Do not turn this flap over or you will turn into an ugly, pimply, vampire with soggy underpants.

'I know,' I say. 'Rocks!'

'Rocks?' says Danny.

'We'll put rocks in her pack! That'll give her something to laugh about.'

'Great idea,' says Danny, 'but how are you going to get the rocks into her pack without her seeing?'

'I'm not going to put the rocks in her pack,' I say. 'You are.'

'Me?' says Danny. 'What if she catches me?'

'She won't,' I say, 'because I'll divert her.'

There are three rocks – each roughly the size of a small coconut – a few metres down the track. I point them out to Danny.

'Those will do.'

'All three of them?' says Danny.

'All three of them,' I say. 'And hide them down the bottom of her pack so she doesn't find them until tonight.'

'Hang on,' says Danny. 'Which one is Roseanne's pack?'

'It's the green one,' I say.

I look around for Roseanne. She's over talking to Derek Watson, the leader of the

Urban Bush Tucker

Fresh butts with french flies.

It was my favorite one too... my right leg.

59

trip. She has her compass out and is pointing towards the ocean. Derek is shaking his head. Her first bushwalk and already she thinks she knows better than the leader! She is really something else.

Roseanne has this brand-new compass, which she hasn't stopped showing everybody for the whole trip. She's got no idea how to use it, but that doesn't stop her telling everybody else how to use theirs. It gives me an idea.

'Hey, Roseanne,' I say. 'Can you give me some help checking my compass? I'm not sure if it's pointing true north or not.'

She's already on her way over. We go back to the boulder and start comparing compasses, taking sightings onto one of the small, rocky islands out from the coast.

I stall her for about ten minutes and then return to the group. Danny nods and winks.

People are getting ready to move. I sit down and slip my arms through the straps of my pack. It weighs a million tonnes. I packed food for four days, but it feels like I've got enough to last for the next four months. Maybe I shouldn't have brought so much canned food.

But I don't mind. No matter how heavy my pack is, Roseanne's must be even heavier.

Not that it seems to be giving her much trouble. She picks it up with one hand, slips her arms through the shoulder straps and strides to the front of the group. She's off down the trail and around the bend before anybody else has even started walking. You'd think Danny had filled her pack with helium balloons.

Even though my legs are feeling like jelly after the morning's climb, I walk quickly to catch up with Roseanne. I want to enjoy the sight of her carrying our rocks. If nothing else, it'll help take my mind off the weight of my own load. No matter how much pain I'm in, she'll be feeling worse.

She's walking so fast that after about fifteen minutes we've left the rest of the group way behind. The track becomes steeper and slightly overgrown. Roseanne pushes her way past a small tree branch that's hanging across the track and holds it back for me.

See! We warned you!!

BUSHWALKING TIP

If you are really sick of walking, try lying down and pretend you've been bitten by a deadly snake. (If someone's got a mobile, you'll get a great helicopter ride).

They want to know what kind of chopper you want.

Left FOOT side, I meant to say

A GUIDE TO COMMON ROCKS FOUND ON BUSH TRAILS

1. A Rock

2. Square Rock

3. Pointy Rock

4. Spotty Rock

5. Small Rock

6. BIG ROCK

7. Flat Rock

8. WOMBAT ROCKS (Edible).

Just as I'm about to grab it, she lets go and the branch flicks back hard against my face. The pain makes my eyes water.

'Watch it,' I say. 'Are you trying to blind me?'

'Sorry about that,' says Roseanne. 'But you should always try to keep at least two metres behind the person in front so that they can't flick branches in your face.'

'I *was* staying behind, but you deliberately held it back for me.'

'That's cos I'm such a nice person,' she says. 'I thought you'd grab it. Honest!'

'Yeah, right, Roseanne.'

She must think I'm stupid. She's staring at me with that silly grin on her face. And, what's worse, she doesn't look the slightest bit tired. There's not a single drop of sweat on her.

'How are you feeling?' I ask.

'Great!' she says. 'How about you?'

'Fine!' I say. 'Never felt better. You've got such a big pack, though. It looks like it must be heavy.'

'Yeah, it's heavy,' she says. 'But I can

62

Now, they've both gone !! ARGHHH!!

handle it. Hey, what's that on your jumper?'

She points to my chest.

I freeze. Please, no, don't let it be a spider. Anything but a spider. I look down and Roseanne flicks her finger up my chin, my nose and off the top of my head.

'Gotcha!' she cackles, as I jerk backwards – which is not a good move, considering how heavy my pack is. The next thing I know I'm falling off the track and crashing through the scrub.

I land in a bramble bush. I can't get up. I'm on my back, just like an upside-down tortoise.

'Enjoy your trip?' calls Roseanne.

'Ha ha. Very funny,' I say.

'Are you all right?'

'I don't know,' I say, 'I can't get up.'

'Hang on,' she says. She shrugs off her pack and slides down the bank. 'Give me your hand.'

The thought of having to hold Roseanne's hand is only marginally more appealing than having to hold a live funnel-web spider, but I'm not exactly in a position to refuse.

63

Her grip is strong and she pulls me up easily.

But I can't put any weight on my left foot. I have to sit straight back down.

'Where does it hurt?' says Roseanne.

'My ankle. I think it's broken.'

'Take your boot off and let's have a look,' she says.

I undo my boot-laces and slip my sock off.

'Yeah, it's pretty swollen,' she says. 'But it's not broken. You're going to need a bandage, though. I've got one in my pack.'

Roseanne climbs back up the bank, grabs her first-aid kit and is back in a flash.

She puts a cream-coloured bandage on the top of my foot and wraps it around twice. Then she winds it around my ankle and back under and over my foot again, in a figure of eight motion.

'Where did you learn to do that?' I ask.

'I'm doing my scout training,' she informs me matter-of-factly.

'I didn't know that,' I say.

'You didn't ask.'

Help. They've just come out my mouth.

At last the others catch up.

'What's going on?' asks Derek, craning his neck to see what we're doing. 'You two playing footsie?'

'He's hurt his ankle,' says Roseanne. 'Pretty bad too.'

'Can he walk?' asks Derek.

'Not properly,' she says. 'But he can lean on her? He won't be able to carry his pack, though. We'll have to unpack it and share the load around.'

How To
Fix A
Blister

Lean on her? Is she crazy? I can't believe what I'm hearing.

'It's okay,' I say. 'I'll be all right.'

But Roseanne's not listening.

She's lugged my pack up to the trail and is distributing its contents amongst the other walkers.

step 1.
step 2. Rub
salt into
wound.

'Hey,' she says. 'What are you carrying these for?'

She's holding up three rocks, each the size of a small coconut.

I don't believe it.

I can't believe it.

I won't believe it.

Get back where you belong!

Could Danny be *that* stupid?

This calls for some quick thinking. I don't want to end up looking like an idiot in front of the whole group.

'I can explain,' I say, trying to act like it's the most normal thing in the world to carry rocks in your pack. 'See, I'm a rock collector and . . .'

But Roseanne is shaking her head.

'Why put the rocks in your pack?' she says. 'Why not carry them in your head with the rest of the collection?'

Everybody starts laughing. Everybody, that is, except me. And Danny. This is all his fault. I should never have trusted him.

If only he had never had the stupid idea of putting rocks in her pack in the first place!

After Roseanne finishes distributing the contents of my pack, she slides back down the bank.

'Put your arm around my neck,' she says. 'I'll help you up.'

My arm? *Her* neck? She's got to be kidding.

'No, it's okay thanks,' I say. 'I think I can walk now.'

A
GUIDE
TO TRACKS
IN THE BUSH

1. DOG

2. Something furry?

3. Gold Fish?

4. Buddhist

5. Merchant Banker

6. Philos- opher.

7. Wombat on a bike

8. Echidna on its back.

66
It's growing back.

'Suit yourself,' she says.

I grab a small tree and start to pull myself up the bank. But the pain in my ankle is too much. I miss my footing and fall backwards.

Roseanne lifts me up, places my arm over her shoulder and helps me up the bank.

She might be annoying, but I've got to hand it to her: she knows how to handle an emergency.

Danny is standing at the side of the trail, looking sheepish.

'Maggot-brained moron!' I hiss at him.

He just shrugs. He knows it's the truth.

As I limp alongside Roseanne, we talk. She tells me that this is the sixth school she's been to.

'You got kicked out of five schools?' I ask.

'I wasn't kicked out,' she says. 'We keep moving. Dad's an engineer. He has to move because of his work. We never stay in one place for more than a year or two.'

'Isn't that hard?' I ask.

'A bit,' she says. 'It's kind of lonely.'

After a long afternoon we've finally made

it to Waterloo Bay. Roseanne hasn't stopped talking and cracking jokes the whole way. Some of them are pretty funny, too.

We're the last ones in. I stagger onto the beach and into the camping area behind the sand-dunes.

'There you go,' says Roseanne. 'How's your ankle feeling?'

'A bit better.'

'Think you'll be all right for tomorrow?'

'I hope so,' I say.

'Well, if not, give me a yell.'

You know, I hate to admit it but, even with all her stupid practical jokes and wisecracks, Roseanne's not so bad. In fact, to tell the truth, I'm kind of starting to like her.

'Thanks, Roseanne. I owe you one.'

'You don't owe me anything,' she says, putting her hand on my shoulder. 'But could you just do me one small favour?'

'What's that?' I say.

She gives me this big cheesy grin and winks.

'Tell your mum I saved you!'

what..?

Emergency spew relish

I t's the last week of school holidays and I'm flying to Mildura to visit my grandparents.

I'm on one of those little thirty-six seater planes.

I've got a window seat, but I want the seat next to me as well. I want to spread out and get comfortable.

I don't think anybody's going to sit there now, but I've laid a piece of rubber dog poo on the seat, just to make sure.

I'm doing really well. It's almost time for take-off and nobody's sat there yet, and there are still two empty seats behind me.

An old lady boards the plane and shuffles down the aisle.

If the plane starts to plummet, do up your seat belt. It won't save your life, but it'll make it easier to find the bodies.

The best PRACTICAL JOKE EVER has been moved. GO TO Pg.9 (nine) NOW!

With a bit of luck, she'll take the seat behind me and then the flight attendant will close the door and I can relax.

But the old lady stops right next to me. I can't believe it.

'No! No! No!' I'm thinking. 'Keep going!'

'Excuse me,' she says, 'is this seat taken?'

'Um, er, no, not exactly,' I say, 'but I don't think I'd sit in it if I was you . . . it's not very clean.'

The old lady bends over and pats the seat. She finds the dog poo, picks it up and strokes it.

'It's only a piece of rubber dog poo,' she says. 'I suppose it's some young person's idea of a joke.'

She puts the poo into an air-sickness bag hanging in front of the seat.

Rubber dogs don't do poo.

Pretty cool old lady. But how did she know it was only rubber? That's the very best quality rubber dog poo money can buy. That stuff even fools my dog.

'So I can sit here, after all,' she says. 'You don't mind, do you?'

I want to say, 'Yes, actually, I do mind!

70

There are plenty of empty seats! Why don't you go and sit in one of them?'

But I don't want to be rude – especially not to an old lady. And I can't just get up and go and sit in one of the empty seats myself, because she might think I'm being nasty. She might be really lonely and not have any friends, and me going to another seat might be the last straw.

It's going to have to be her who moves.

She puts her handbag underneath her seat and settles in with a can of Kool Mints.

This is going to require some pretty quick thinking.

At last the doors are shut and the flight attendant welcomes us on board. She points out the emergency exits and life-jackets and oxygen masks. Some welcome, but it does give me an idea.

The engines start up and fill the plane with their low vibrations.

'I hope it's not too rough a ride,' I say, 'because I'm a hopeless air traveller. I practically get sick even *thinking* about planes.'

'What?' she says. 'You'll have to speak up!'

I lean close to her old wrinkled ear.

'I said, I'm a hopeless air traveller! I always get sick on planes.'

The old lady smiles.

'That's good then,' she says. 'We can look after each other. I'm not much of a one for air travel either!'

Oh great. Just lovely. Not only does she take up my seat, now she's threatening to get sick all over me as well.

The plane shudders and moves forward with a groan.

Take-off is my favourite part.

The captain's voice comes over the speakers:

'Good morning and thank you for flying with Southern Australia Airlines. We have almost perfect conditions for our flight this morning. We'll be cruising at around five thousand metres, at a speed of five hundred kilometres per hour. We have a slight tail wind and we expect to reach our destination in just under an hour. We hope you have a

We just fill up wit gas

Now they're turning into wheels!

pleasant flight.'

'What did he say?' says the lady. 'What did he say?'

'He said it's going to be pretty rough,' I tell her. 'Hurricanes and tornadoes are expected. He said to hold tight and just hope and pray that you're not sitting next to someone who's prone to air-sickness. He said that it's okay if you want to change seats when the plane stops climbing in a few minutes.'

And float away

'Well, I'm not going to change seats,' says the lady. 'I feel very lucky that I'm sitting next to a big, strong young man like you. I'd be too scared to sit by myself in conditions like this.'

The plane finishes its long slow taxi out to the runway. It turns and then starts rushing forward. I can feel my body being drawn back hard against the seat as the wheels leave the tarmac and we climb steeply into the sky.

Great landing, Hal.

The pilot is right, of course. It's one of the smoothest take-offs ever. But I jiggle and shake and rattle the seats to make it seem really wild and rough.

73

Wow, getting mobile at last

'Ooohhh,' I groan. 'Oooooohhhhh. I feel sick already. Are you sure you don't want to change seats?'

'No, love,' she says, taking my hand in hers. 'I'll look after you.'

Oh no! What did I do to deserve this? Now she wants to be my mother!

This calls for serious evasive action.

Forget the emergency life-jackets and the emergency oxygen masks. They are absolutely no use to me.

This situation calls for the emergency corn relish.

Actually, I don't call corn relish 'corn relish'. I call it 'spew relish'. Because, as far as I'm concerned, the only difference between corn relish and spew is that corn relish comes in a jar.

It looks like spew.

It smells like spew.

It even tastes like spew.

The only thing more like spew than corn relish is custard, and I don't even want to think about that because it will *really* make me spew.

from piranha to Porsche!

Anyway, I always carry a jar of spew relish with me for emergencies just like this.

I slide my hand out of the old lady's.

'It's okay now, thank you,' I say. 'I'm feeling much better all of a sudden.'

'Well, you just let me know if there's anything I can do for you,' she says.

The flight attendant unbuckles herself from her seat and starts her mad rush to offer us all drinks and food. The flight usually only lasts about an hour. As soon as she's finished giving out teas, coffees, fruit juices, cans of drink and biscuits in cellophane, it'll be time to collect all the left-overs, pack everything up and strap herself back into her seat, ready for landing.

She approaches our seat.

The old lady orders a cup of tea and biscuits. I want to order one of everything, but I can't. For the old spew relish trick to work, I've got to convince her that I'm too sick to eat.

'Nothing for me, thank you,' I say.

The flight attendant returns with the tea. While the old lady's busy adding her sugar and milk, I reach down to my bag and dig out my jar of spew relish.

By the time I'm through, this old lady is not going to want to sit next to me.

She's not going to even want to sit on the same plane as me.

In fact, I'll make sure she never even wants to *go* on a plane again.

I'm bent over, facing the window so the old lady can't see what I'm doing. I screw the lid off the jar. I pinch my nose and tip the jar of spew relish up to my mouth. I try to suck in as much as I can without swallowing. I manage to get about half the jar in. Lucky I've got such a big mouth.

I put the lid on the jar and tuck it back into my bag.

I sit back in my seat, hold my belly and moan quietly.

'Are you all right?' says the old lady.

I can't answer, of course, because my mouth's full.

I just groan, louder this time.

'Do you need a sick bag?' she says.

I nod.

She grabs a bag from in front of her – the one with my rubber dog poo in it – and passes it to me.

I rock back and forth and puff out my cheeks and then pretend to splurk up into the bag. Not that it all goes into the bag, of course.

I take care to dribble some down my chin and onto my T-shirt.

'Oh, you poor thing,' says the old lady. 'You poor old thing.'

Huh? *She's* calling *me* old?

'I'm okay now, thanks,' I say. 'That feels much better.'

'You know, it's funny,' she says, 'but I'm not feeling sick at all. This is one of the smoothest flights I've ever had. You must have a very delicate stomach.'

'Extremely delicate,' I say. 'But I'm really hungry now.'

'Oh, what a pity,' she says. 'You're too late to order any morning tea.'

'That's okay,' I say. 'I brought my own. Could I borrow your teaspoon?'

'Why certainly,' she says. 'Here you are.'

AMAZING EYE TRICK #3 ANSWER

If you have done this amazing trick correctly, you should now be looking at the back of my living room. AMAZING!

May I borrow your hand bag?

TA.

77

I take the teaspoon. This is it. Any minute now she'll be out of her seat like a rocket.

'Well, down the hatch.'

I open the neck of the sick bag and dip the spoon in. I scoop up a spoonful of spew relish and pull it out of the bag. I pass the spoon under my nose a couple of times and sniff deeply.

'Ahhh!' I say, smiling. 'I love it when it's nice and warm and fresh!'

I open my mouth very slowly. I put the teaspoon on my tongue and close my mouth. Then I slowly draw the teaspoon out and lick it clean, making sure I get every last drop. I close my eyes and sigh, as if I'm in heaven.

I open my eyes. I expect to see the seat next to me empty. I expect the old lady to be as far away from me as possible, and warning everybody else to stay away too.

But the seat is not empty.

The old lady is still there. Still watching.

'Was that nice?' she asks.

'It was beautiful,' I say. 'Tasted even better going down than it did coming up.'

'That's nice,' she says. 'I'm glad. Have

some more.'

What?

If she'd said, 'Let's take our clothes off and run up and down the aisle,' I would only have been half as surprised.

'Um, okay, thanks. I will.'

I eat another spoonful. Only this time I finish with a big belch.

'Excuse me,' I say.

'Oh, don't mention it,' says the old lady. 'In some countries it's good manners to burp after a meal. It's considered a compliment to the cook.'

This old lady is unshakeable. If she thinks this is normal, I'd hate to see mealtimes at her house.

I'm going to have to take this prank to the next level.

I get another spoonful and, instead of putting it in my mouth, I plonk it on top of my head.

'Makes great shampoo, too,' I say. 'Or should I say "sham-spew"?'

The old lady just nods.

I load up my spoon again, and this time I

splatter spew relish all over my face. I rub it into my eyes, my cheeks, my ears.

'I reckon it's just a great all-round beauty cream,' I say. 'Do you find that gross?'

The old lady just looks on, a slight smile on her face.

'No,' she says calmly. 'In fact, I'd love to try some of this amazing food that doubles as a beauty cream. What do you call it?'

The penny drops.

I hold up three fingers in front of her face.

'How many fingers am I holding up?' I ask her.

She pauses.

'I don't know, dear. I'm blind. Why do you ask?'

'No reason,' I say, trying not to gag from the stench of the spew relish, which I just know I'm not going to be able to get out of my skin and hair for months. 'No reason at all. But I think I'm going to be sick again.'

'Oh, you poor thing,' says the old lady, passing me another sick bag. 'You poor old thing.'

BEAT THE BOMB!

Danny and I are about to play the best practical joke in history. We've been working on it all morning. We owe the idea to my mum.

Mum listens to the radio non-stop. It's always on. Wouldn't be so bad if she listened to something good, like Triple R, but she prefers the golden-oldie station Triple B. The B stands for Boredom. Talk about sad music. It's so sad and boring they have to run competitions all the time to bribe people to listen to it.

They've got this competition at the moment called Beat the Bomb. Every hour they ring up a listener and then start the clock ticking. Every few seconds, over the sound of the clock, a voice says ever-increasing amounts of money, like 'One thousand dollars . . . one thousand and fifty-five dollars . . . two thousand and three dollars . . . ' and so on. The listener has to tell the DJ when to stop, and if they do it before the bomb explodes, then they get to keep that amount of money. It can last anywhere from a couple of seconds to half a minute.

The trick is having the nerve to let the clock tick for as long as possible. I've never heard anyone with enough nerve to win more than a few thousand dollars.

All you have to do to be in it is send your name and phone number to Triple B. If they select you they ring you and you get a chance to play.

I've entered about fifteen times. I reckon that makes me fifteen times more likely to win. I don't think anybody else would be clever enough to have thought of that.

But in the meantime – while I wait for

82

them to call – Danny and I are going to have some fun. We've recorded the station signature tune, a couple of advertisements and a couple of songs. And I can do a pretty convincing imitation of a DJ when I try. We're going to ring Brian Bortello and pretend that he's about to play Beat the Bomb.

Why Brian Bortello? Because we always play jokes on Brian Bortello.

'Let's do it,' says Danny. 'It's ten past four.'

'Okay,' I say. I pick up the receiver and start punching the buttons.

Danny is laughing.

'Hey, shut up,' I say. 'It's ringing!'

'Hello?'

It's a woman speaking. Must be his mother.

'Hello – it's Chris Robbins from Triple B FM,' I say in my radio voice. 'Could I speak to Brian Bortello please?'

'Yes, just a minute.'

'Brian!' she calls. 'Telephone!'

'He'll be with you in a minute,' she says. 'Brian!'

Finally he picks up the phone.

'Hello?'

'Brian Bortello?'

'Yes.'

'Chris Robbins from Triple B FM here. How are you doing?'

'Good thanks . . . What did you say your name was?'

...and some grilled flake -.

'Chris Robbins. Your name's been drawn this hour to play Beat the Bomb.'

'Beat the what?'

'Beat the Bomb!'

'What's that?'

DUE TO UNFORSEEN CIRCUMSTANCES the best practical joke ever is now on:
1. Female version Pg.111.
2. Male version Pg. 125.

'You know, our competition. You should know – you entered it.'

'I don't remember doing that.'

'Well, maybe a friend did it for you. Would you like to have a go?'

'Yeah, I guess so,' he says.

'Well, stand by, we're about to go to air. I'll just play a couple of ads and a station ID and then you're on. Oh, and by the way, Brian?'

'Yes?'

84

'Turn your radio off. We will be transmitting on a ten-second delay and it can get very confusing.'

I point at Danny. He starts playing a jingle for Cheapies carpet-cleaning service right next to my phone.

'I think we've got him!' I whisper to Danny.

The carpet ad finishes and one for a supermarket starts. Then the Triple B station ID comes on. It sounds really spacey – like comets and meteorites whizzing past your ears.

'Triple B – taking you back to the good old days . . . ' says the voice-over. The sound of the meteorites ends in a shower of xylophone notes. It's the only exciting sound on the whole station.

'Good afternoon,' I say. 'Chris Robbins with you on Triple B, and to play Beat the Bomb this hour we have Brian Bortello on the line. How are you doing, Brian?'

'Good, thanks.'

'Great! What are you up to this afternoon?'

PARTS OF THE BODY # 121

The finger.
(Really a crocodile pretending)

I'm bored.

85

'Nothing much, you know.'

'Fantastic! Ready to play?'

'Yes.'

'All right – now, you know the rules, Brian?'

'No,' he says.

'I'm going to start the clock ticking. You say stop when you think you've won enough, and it's yours to keep. But don't leave it too late. If the bomb explodes, you end up empty-handed!'

AMAZING
EYE
TRICKS #4:
Stare at
the space
between
these shapes.

Does it
remind
you of
anything?
Ans: Pg 102

'Yeah, I've got it,' he says.

'Okay. Clock's ticking.'

Danny plays the next bit of the recording.

tick tick tick tick tick tick tick

He picks up a cardboard tube and puts one end to the phone and the other to his mouth.

'Twenty dollars,' he says. The tube gives his voice the spacey echo of the real voice. It's this sort of attention to detail that makes our practical jokes so special.

tick tick tick tick tick tick tick

Brian says nothing.

my impression
of a double
ended fish.

'One thousand and sixty-three dollars,'
says Danny, obviously enjoying himself.

'Three thousand and fifteen dollars.'

Silence. This guy's got nerves of steel.
Either that or he's really greedy. Most people
would have bailed out by now.

'Three thousand and eighty-three dollars.'

Danny looks at me. I shrug.

'Four thousand and forty-four dollars!'
says Danny.

tick tick tick tick tick tick tick

'Five thousand dollars.'

'Stop!' says Brian.

I signal to Danny to stop the recording.

'Brian?'

'Yes?'

'Do you know what you've just done?'

'No, did I do something wrong?'

'Wrong? Brian, you have just won five
thousand dollars! What do you think about
that?'

'Wow! That's fantastic! I can't believe it!'
he says. 'Mum – I just won five thousand
dollars!'

A hammerhead
shark

Brian's mother starts squealing in the background. She's so loud, I have to hold the phone away from my ear. Danny can hear it too. He's rolling around on the floor killing himself laughing.

'Hey, Brian,' I say. 'What are you going to do with all that money?'

'I don't know,' says Brian. 'I don't know. I've never won anything like this!'

Are you UGLY. Now Dr. Griffith's Corrective Surgery can end your embarrassment.

TRY THIS,
↓

'Well congratulations, Brian. Now, if you can stay on the line while we get some details, Elton John is going to take us back and show us how to do the Crocodile Rock. This is Triple B FM where – like Brian Bortello – we make your dreams come true. Good on ya, Brian!'

OR THIS,↓

'Thanks!' he says.

Danny starts playing 'Crocodile Rock'.

We're about to yell, 'Just kidding!' when I hear a strange sound on the other end of the line. Like somebody crying

I can hear Brian talking.

OR THIS.
↓

'It's okay, Mum, it's okay. You should be happy!'

A parrot fish.

'I am happy,' she says.

Why would she be crying?

Danny's laughing so hard I can barely hear them.

'Shhh!' I tell him.

'What's wrong?' he says.

'I'm not sure,' I tell him. 'Just keep the noise down.'

Danny screws up his face.

'Brian, are you still there?' I say.

'Yeah, sorry, Mum's a bit emotional.'

'That's completely understandable,' I say. 'Five thousand dollars is a lot of money.'

'Yeah,' says Brian. 'Especially for us . . . see . . . since Dad died we've been really struggling. Mum has to work pretty long hours. This money is really going to help out. You've got no idea how much it means to us.'

As Brian talks I feel worse and worse. How was I to know his dad died? He didn't say anything. Not that he would have told me – I don't know him that well. But someone could have said something.

89
A flathead.

'Yeah, um, glad to be able to help out, Brian. Now if I could just get your address...'

Well, what else can I say? Somehow, 'Just kidding!' doesn't seem quite as funny as it did a few minutes ago.

Danny's stopped laughing. He's frowning at me.

'What are you doing?' he says.

I wave him away with my hand.

I take down Brian's address.

'Thanks, Brian. We'll send you a letter in the next few days with details of how to collect your payment.'

'Chris,' says Brian, 'can I just say that you've made me and my mum really happy today – thanks a lot.'

'Don't mention it,' I say, and hang up.

'Are you out of your mind?' says Danny.

'His dad died.'

'So?'

'They really need the money.'

'So you promised it to them?'

I nod.

'Oh, man ... ' Danny is shaking his head.

Are you waiting to see the SCHOOL PRINCIPAL?

Then, try eating his indoor plants to stumps. He'll be very impressed

I'm still bored

'His mother was crying,' I say. 'He said she's been working really hard. I couldn't tell them it was just a joke. I couldn't.'

'So, you're going to send him five thousand dollars because you feel bad about a little practical joke.'

'It's not a *little* practical joke,' I say. 'It's a BIG mistake!'

'Know what I think?' says Danny.

'What?'

'Just do nothing. That way there's no need to explain. There's nothing to trace it back to us.'

'But what if they ring the radio station?'

'The radio station won't know anything about it,' says Danny. 'Brian will realise it was a joke.'

'But that's terrible!' I say. 'Think how he'll feel. That's even worse than admitting it was a hoax. After all they've been through! No – we've got to get them that money.'

'What do you propose? Rob a bank?'

'No – we'll wash cars, mow lawns, pool all our pocket-money – and then we'll invest it

Don't turn this next page or I'll explode

91

KICK ME

in a high-interest bank account. We'll have
the money in no time.'

'We?' says Danny.

'What do you mean?' I say.

'*You* made the call.'

'*You* helped me.'

'But it was your idea.'

'You didn't say no.'

Danny hits himself on the head with his
open palm. 'Do you have any idea how many
cars we'll have to wash to earn that much
money?!'

The phone rings.

I pick it up.

'Hello.'

'Hi, could I speak to Andy Griffiths?'

'Speaking.'

'Hi, Andy. Chris Robbins from Triple B
FM here.'

Oh no! He must have found out I've been
impersonating him! Brian must have rung
him back to check if the call was for real!
When he found out it was a trick he would
have guessed it was me.

Just
KIDDING!

92

'Who is it?' says Danny.

I put my hand over the phone. 'It's Chris Robbins! He must know! What do I do?'

'Talk to him,' says Danny. 'He can't prove anything.'

CUP DAY,
the year
2000.

'Andy?' says Chris. 'Are you still there?'

'Yes,' I say. 'I'm here.'

'Thought we'd lost you for a minute.'

'Just a bit surprised,' I say. 'What can I do for you?'

'Well,' says Chris, 'You've just been selected to play Beat the Bomb – but if you'd rather not . . .'

..And still
Phar Lap
brings up
the year...

'Are you kidding?' I shout. 'Of course I want to!'

It's like a dream. What are the odds of something like this happening? A million to one? Nah – more like a zillion to one.

'Well, stand by,' says Chris. 'We're about to go to air. I'll just play a couple of ads and a station ID and then you're on. Oh, and by the way, Andy?'

'Yes?'

'Turn your radio off. We will be

Don't turn the page ... or I'll turn into an electrical appliance.

KICK ME

transmitting on a ten-second delay and it can get a little confusing.'

I hear the jingle for Cheapies carpet-cleaning service. Talk about deja vu. If Danny wasn't right next to me I'd swear it was him playing another prank.

Then the Triple B station ID starts. Comets and meteorites again. 'Triple B – taking you back to the good old days . . .'

Then Chris starts speaking.

'Good afternoon. Chris Robbins with you on Triple B, and to play Beat the Bomb this hour we have Andy on the line. How are you doing, Andy?'

'Pretty good.'

'Great! What are you up to this afternoon?'

I wonder what he would say if I told him I was impersonating him and making prank Beat the Bomb phone calls. But I decide against it. I need the cash.

'Nothing much, you know.'

'Fantastic! Ready to play Beat the Bomb?'

'I sure am.'

'All right – now, you know the rules, Andy?'

PARTS
of
The
BODY.

NO. 15

BIG TOE,
with trapdoor
to allow
the bone
to get out
for a
smoko
every now
and
then.

94

'Yes,' I say, but he explains them anyway.

'Okay. Clock's ticking,' says Chris.

'Twenty dollars,' says the voice from outer space

tick tick tick tick tick tick tick

I'd be happy with twenty. Maybe I should stop it right now. Those bombs can go off pretty fast sometimes.

'Twenty-five dollars.'

tick tick tick tick tick tick tick

'One thousand and forty-eight dollars.'

I want to stop, but I can't. It's like I'm frozen. If I can just keep my nerve . . .

'Two thousand and ninety dollars.'

tick tick tick tick tick tick tick

'Four thousand and sixty-six dollars.'

The ticking is deafening. Any minute now the bomb is going to explode and I'll be splattered all over the room. But still I can't speak.

'Five thousand and two dollars.'

I can't stand it anymore.

'Stop!' I yell.

'Andy?'

HEALTH TIP.
If your brain starts leaking out of your ear, place an old cork in your earhole and hammer it in.

95

Your toast's ready.

KICK ME

'Yes?'

'Do you know what you've just done?'

'Yes,' I say in a dream.

'You have just won five thousand and two dollars! What do you think about that?'

I can't speak.

Danny's jumping up and down.

'How much?' he's saying. 'How much?!'

'Five thousand and two,' I say.

Danny hoots.

'Hey, Andy,' says Chris. 'What are you going to do with all that money?'

A vision of me sitting on top a pile of money as high as Mount Everest fills my head. But then I think of Brian. And his mother.

'I'm not sure,' I say. 'Maybe I'll give it to a friend.'

Danny raises his eyebrows.

'Well, good for you, Andy,' says Chris. 'Now, if you can stay on the line while we confirm your details, we've got something special coming up. Do you like John Farnham, Andy?'

An old
piece of
wood

(Ask yourself,
"Where has
it come from?")

Didn't I ask
you not to turn the
page?

96

I can't stand him, but I'll say anything for five thousand and two bucks.

'*Like* him? I *love* him!' I lie.

'Well, this is for you mate,' he says over the start of 'You're the Voice'. 'This is Triple B FM where – like Andy – we make your dreams, and your friends' dreams, come true. Good on ya, Andy!'

'Thanks,' I say.

My head is spinning. I'm trying to work out if I'm the most fantastically lucky person or the biggest loser in the world. I mean, having to pretend I like John Farnham is bad enough, but having one of his songs dedicated to me is much, much worse.

BATTERIES

BATTERY
HEN
↓

'Are you going to give that money to me?' says Danny. He's practically drooling all over the carpet.

'No,' I say. 'What makes you think that?'

'You said you were going to give it to a friend.'

'Yes, but not you,' I say.

'Then who?'

'Brian.'

Don't turn the
page or I'll turn
into a septic Tank.

KICK
ME

His jaw drops.

'You're kidding!'

'No,' I say.

'All of it?'

'No, not all of it. After I pay Brian what we owe him there will be two dollars left over. We can go halves in that if you like.'

'Thanks,' says Danny, staring at the carpet. 'You're a real pal.'

'Don't mention it,' I say. 'What are friends for?'

WOW!! I've been run over by a HONDA 750cc...

So you think a Cockroach has an I.Q. of 120, oh? That'd make me twice as smart as you. Try again.

HA. HA. HA Tricked You!!

98

Born to Die

Well, I finally did it.

I've been thinking about it for ages and I kept putting it off, but this morning I finally did it.

I got a tattoo.

It's a skull with two eagle wings curving up over the top. The skull has these evil green eyes and a sort of long, thin red moustache that curls upwards next to the wings. And running across the bottom of the skull is a small ribbon-shaped banner. And inside the banner are the words BORN TO DIE.

Didn't cost much either. Normally, it would have cost $2.95, but I got it on special for ninety-five cents.

And the best thing about it is that it didn't even hurt.

I just removed the protective sheet and pressed the sticky side firmly onto my skin. Then I wet the top of it with a sponge, waited for thirty seconds and peeled off the backing.

Yeah, so it's not a real tattoo – but it's so realistic you'd never know the difference. And the amazing thing is, it makes me feel different. Bigger. Tougher. Bolder. Nobody's going to want to kick sand in my face and steal my girlfriend when they see I've got such a scary-looking tat. Not that I have a girlfriend right at the moment, but as soon as they see my tattoo I bet every girl in school will want to go out with me – even the teachers.

The packet says it will last for days – almost forever. It also says I'll be able to shock my friends and family. But it's not my friends and family I'm interested in shocking. It's my enemies: Harry Leak and Sean Leech.

Harry Leak lives at the bottom of the

hill. He's a few years older than me, but we used to hang around a bit together on the weekends. Until he started hanging around with Sean Leech.

Sean Leech lives over on the other side of the hill. He's got a face like a rat, with a really thin pointy nose and beady brown eyes. He doesn't like me much. Well, to be truthful, he hates my guts. I don't know what I did to make him hate me so much. Being born I suppose. Sean Leech is just that sort of guy.

I hate your guts.

Lately, him and Harry have taken to waiting for me at the bottom of the hill outside Harry's house and they won't let me pass until I tell them the password. Today is no exception. I turn the corner into my street and they're both there, like they've been waiting for me. Sean is sitting in the middle of the footpath. Harry is leaning against his letterbox with a yellow bucket in his hand. I could try crossing the road, but I know they'd just come after me. I pretend to ignore them.

'Well, well, well,' says Sean. 'If it isn't our old mate Andy.'

How to impress your school PRINCIPAL.

Wrap masking tape around your face and pretend to be his mummy.

101

I think I'll eat it.

Harry smirks.

'Do you mind if I just go past?' I say, moving to step around him. But Sean's hand shoots out and grabs my ankle.

'Not so fast,' he says. 'Say please.'

'Please,' I say, looking straight ahead.

'Say "pretty please",' he says. '"With sugar on top".'

'Pretty please with sugar on top,' I say.

'Say "pretty please with sugar on top, Sir!"'

I know from experience that this can go on for a long time. But today I don't have to put up with this because I've got a tattoo. I casually roll up my sleeves. The tattoo is still there on my right forearm. The skull's eyes seem to be flashing.

'Look, I don't want any trouble,' I say. 'Just let me past . . . or else.'

Sean laughs. He hasn't noticed my tattoo yet. But I can see that Harry has. He's already backing away.

'Come on, Sean. That'll do,' he says.

Sean stops laughing. 'Huh?'

Harry steps across to him and whispers in his ear.

Sean jumps up from the footpath, his eyes fixed on my forearm. He takes a couple of steps backwards.

'Can I pass now?' I ask.

'Yeah, of c-course,' says Sean. 'We were just kidding around. Just a bit of fun, you know.'

'Fun?' I say. 'That's what you call fun?'

Sean and Harry are standing there frozen, like a couple of stunned rabbits. I'm not sure whether they're scared of the tattoo or just the way it makes me act, but I don't really care. I flex the muscles in my forearm – which is a hard thing to do really, because I don't have that many. But my skull doesn't mind. It ripples and seems to grin in response, like it's enjoying it. I feel strangely calm. Like I can do whatever I want. Why not pull out all the stops and teach them a lesson they'll never forget?

Harry is still holding the yellow bucket.

'What's in the bucket?' I say.

'Slugs,' says Harry.

'Why?' I ask, knowing full well that their idea of fun is inventing new and horrible

If you turn this page, your undies will fall down, your nose will drop off and all your hair will fall out. And you will start barking like a dog.

You know perfectly well there's a hook there.

ways for slugs to die.

'Um, er, well, my dad asked me to collect them,' says Harry. 'They've been eating his rose bushes.'

'Don't give me that,' I say. 'Let them go.'

Harry looks at Sean. Sean nods. Harry tips the bucket, and about twenty fat grey slugs fall into the shrubbery.

I watch them helplessly trying to untangle themselves from one another and shake my head.

'You know,' I say, 'maybe it's just me, but I don't find that very funny.'

Harry and Sean are both silent.

'And another thing I don't find very funny is you two making me say a password every time I try to walk past your house. It's got to stop.'

'Sorry,' says Harry. 'No hard feelings. How about a milkshake to make up for it?'

I should leave it here and just keep walking up the hill, but I'm enjoying my new-found power too much. I remember the great milkshakes that Harry used to make for me back in the days when we were friends.

104
I could be caught

SEE, We warned you!!

Two heaped teaspoons of malt, ice-cream and about half a bottle of chocolate syrup. Hardly any room for the milk. Delicious.

'Thought you'd never ask,' I say.

'Okay,' says Harry. 'I'll go get you one, won't be a sec.'

'No, not takeaway,' I say. 'I think I'll drink it inside, if that's okay with you. Sun's kind of hot today.'

Sean and Harry look at each other.

skeleton staff →

'Yeah, Andy,' says Harry. 'Of course. Come in.'

We start walking up the drive. I'm so tough I can't believe it.

Inside, I pick the best seat in the lounge and plonk my feet up on the coffee table. There's a pile of magazines on top of the table, so I push them all off onto the carpet with my feet.

'I think I'll just wait here while you make my milkshake,' I say.

'Sure, fine,' says Harry.

I grab the remote and turn on the television. I turn the sound up so loud that it distorts.

Dragged out of the water

Harry pokes his head around the door.

'Hey, Andy!' he says.

'What?'

'Can you turn that down a bit?'

'No,' I say. 'I like it loud.'

Harry just stands there like he's not sure whether to rip the remote out of my hand and shove it down my throat or just let it go.

'Wanna make something of it?' I say.

'No,' he says, 'of course not. You're the guest. What flavour milkshake would you like?'

'Chocolate, of course,' I say.

'Coming up,' he says and goes back into the kitchen.

Goodnight
frank.
See you
same time
next week.

I start flicking through the channels on the remote. 'Playschool' on Channel Two. The presenters are pretending to be kookaburras. They're singing a song.

'Kookaburra sits on the old gum tree, merry merry king of the bush is he . . . '

I know exactly how that kookaburra feels. I'm the king and Harry and Sean are my subjects. They will do anything I tell them

Beaten to death
with a bit of wood.

to. I watch a bit more of 'Playschool', then turn it off.

'What's taking so long?' I call.

'Almost ready,' yells Sean.

I hear the high-pitched whine of the blender. My mouth starts watering. Harry's milkshakes are really something else.

The blender stops.

'I don't want it in the container, either,' I say. 'I want it in a glass. With a straw!'

'Coming right up,' calls Harry.

Nearly there.

OUCH!

SIMPSON and his Echidna.

A really tough bloke

Sean comes into the room with the milkshake on a tray. Harry is right behind him.

Sean places the tray on top of the coffee table. The milkshake is in one of those old-fashioned glasses with ridges down the side and a crazy straw sticking out of it. There is a scoop of chocolate ice-cream sitting on top.

Harry picks up the glass and gives it to me. Then they both kneel down on either side of my chair and stare at me.

'Do you mind not staring at me?' I say.

'Sorry,' says Sean, his lips curling into

107

Scaled, filleted, cooked and eaten.

a slight smile. 'We just want to watch you drink it.'

'Yeah,' says Harry. 'We just want to watch you enjoy it.'

There's something about the way he says 'enjoy' that I don't like.

I push my arm forward to make sure they remember who's boss here. I look at them, look at my tattoo and look back at them to make sure they've got the message.

But they just start laughing.

'Would you mind telling me what's so funny?' I say.

'Should we?' says Harry.

'Yes,' says Sean. 'I think we should.'

Sean pulls up his sleeve. Harry pulls up his sleeve.

On each of their arms – in almost exactly the same place as mine – is a skull with green eyes and a long red moustache.

I look at them.

They look at me.

The room is very quiet.

'Well, drink up,' says Harry. 'We're waiting.'

Then who'd tell you what page number it is.

'Um,' I say, 'look, thanks for the milkshake and everything, but I'm not really that thirsty. I might just get going.'

I sit forward to get up, but Harry pushes me back into my seat.

WAITING FOR THE PRINCIPAL?

Charm him by swallowing all the school Goldfish.

'After we've gone to all this trouble? Surely you've got a minute just to drink a milkshake. You can't waste it.'

'Okay,' I say. 'But then I've really got to get going.'

'Sure,' says Harry. 'Drink up.'

I guess there are worse punishments.

I put the glass up to my lips.

'Oh, there's just one thing,' says Sean. 'Hope you don't mind, but we couldn't find any chocolate syrup.'

I'm starting to sweat.

'That's okay,' I say, trying to keep cool. 'What did you use instead?'

'Slugs,' says Sean. 'Now drink up.'

Invisipills

Mrs Wharton is stomping around the library. She's telling kids off for talking. She's telling kids off for leaning back on their chairs. She's practically telling kids off for breathing. You name it, she's telling them off for it.

I reckon she's wasted as a librarian. Mrs Wharton should have been the governor of a high-security prison. That'd be one prison where they wouldn't have to worry about the prisoners talking, leaning back on their chairs or returning their library books late.

The only person Mrs Wharton has not told off so far this lesson is me. That's because I'm working so hard. It's pretty rare

Hi! I've just taken an invisipi

for me to work this hard, but I have a big assignment on Antarctic explorers due in on Monday. It's worth 50 per cent of our end of year mark and I've only just started it.

The trouble is Danny is sitting at the desk next to mine and he keeps going on and on about how he wants to be invisible. He won't shut up. Normally I wouldn't mind, but I don't want to risk getting kicked out of the library because I need to do the research for my project.

'Psst! Andy!' says Danny. 'If I got a can of spray-paint and painted myself pink and painted my whole room pink and everything in it pink – do you think I'd be invisible then?'

'Well, maybe,' I whisper. 'As long as you stayed in your room. But once you left, you'd be a bit conspicuous.'

'Oh,' he says.

He's quiet for a few seconds. Then he leans over again.

'Psst!'

'What!?' I say.

'What does "conspicuous" mean?'

I'm sorry there's been a mistake You should have been directed to pg. 49 Good Luck!!

'It means you wouldn't be invisible anymore! Now would you shut up and do some work – and stop interrupting me!'

'Yeah, sorry,' he says. 'But honestly, do you reckon it would work?'

'For the last time, shut up!'

I reach into my pencil case for a lolly. Well, they're *supposed* to be lollies. They're really just little multi-coloured balls with no taste. Nobody likes these lollies, except three-year-olds – and that's only because they don't know any better. I'm only eating them because they were a present from my gran. It would have been rude to throw them away.

I crunch one between my teeth.

Danny leans over.

'What are those?' he says.

Suddenly I have an idea of how to get rid of him.

Mrs Wharton is up at the loans counter checking out some books. This gives me a few minutes.

'Danny, what would you say if I told you I had a way of *really* making you invisible?'

'How?'

I pass him the tube of lollies.

'I was waiting until your birthday to give you these, but since you want to be invisible so badly, you might as well have them now.'

'What are they?' he says.

'They're *invisipills*. They will make you invisible.'

'For real?'

'Absolutely.'

'Where'd you get them?' he says.

'I made them in science. I got the recipe online.'

Great Places to HIDE!

Danny hits his head with his hand. 'Oh, man! Why didn't I think of that! Which site?'

'I'd rather not say. The recipe was smuggled out of the Pentagon. Top-secret stuff. I could get into a lot of trouble if I'm caught.'

'Have you tried them?'

'Yep.'

'And?'

'They're pretty amazing. One pill will make you completely invisible for about half an hour.'

'Wow! How come you didn't tell me?'

'Like I said, I was keeping it as a surprise for your birthday.'

'Can I try one?'

'Sure. Just one, though. They're pretty powerful. And you've got to promise me one thing.'

'What?' says Danny.

'That after you've taken it you'll go outside and let me work.'

'No problem,' he says.

He takes a lolly from the tube.

His eyes are wide as he puts it onto his tongue, closes his mouth and swallows.

'Well?' he says. 'Am I invisible?'

'Not yet,' I say. 'It takes a few minutes.'

Danny's holding his hands out in front of him, fingers out-stretched.

'Have I faded even a little bit?' he says. 'What do you reckon?'

I screw up my eyes, pretending to study him.

'Yes – definitely!' I say. 'No doubt about it.'

'Cool!' he says.

I glance up. Mrs Wharton has finished

at the loans counter and is prowling the library again.

'You're fading fast now,' I say. 'I can hardly see you.'

'No I'm not,' he says. 'I can still see me as clear as anything.'

'Yeah – you're meant to. That's the way the pills are designed. You can see yourself, but nobody can see you. If you couldn't see yourself, you wouldn't know where you were and you'd get lost.'

'Oh, I get it,' he says. 'So, am I invisible yet?'

'Where are you?'

'I'm right here!'

'No you're not. Not as far as I can see. Your chair is empty.'

'Can you still hear me?'

'Yes. Now go outside! Remember our deal?'

'Okay,' says Danny. 'Here I go.'

Danny gets up out of his seat and walks away.

Mrs Wharton is coming slowly towards me.

I go back to my assignment and do my best imitation of a serious student.

Just as she's walking past my desk I hear the most enormous burp.

It's so loud it practically shakes the foundations of the library.

For a moment I think it was Mrs Wharton. But that – of course – is ridiculous. Only Danny can do them that loud.

Great Places to Hide.

I look around. Sure enough, Danny is killing himself laughing in the aisle.

Mrs Wharton stops.

'Excuse me!' she says. 'Was that you?'

'No, Mrs Wharton,' I say.

'Then who was it, pray tell? A ghost?'

'I don't know, Mrs Wharton. But it wasn't me.'

'I don't believe you. What are those?' she says, pointing at the lollies, which Danny has thoughtfully left sitting on my desk in full view.

'Um . . . lollies, Mrs Wharton.'

'I presume you know the rule about eating in the library.'

'Yes, Mrs Wharton.'

'And you know that it specifically excludes chewing gum, bubble gum *and* lollies?'

'Yes, Mrs Wharton. I'll get rid of them.'

'No you won't,' she says, '*I* will.'

She holds out her hand. I pick up the tube and give it to her. Little does she realise she's doing me a big favour.

She walks on up the aisle without another word.

That was close. I'm going to kill Danny after school. With any luck, he's kept his promise and is outside by now.

Thump!

A book lands on the carpet next to my desk. It's *The Wonderful World of Freshwater Fish*, and I have no doubt who threw it.

Another book sails over the top of the shelves and lands on my desk. Whack! Another hits the top edge of the desk and bounces off onto the student in front of me.

Great Places to Hide.

'Ouch!' she yells, turning to me. 'Quit it!'

'It wasn't me,' I say.

The books keep coming. And so does Mrs Wharton.

'Stand up!' she says. 'Would you mind

No, I was.

telling me what's going on here?'

'Somebody is throwing books over the tops of the shelves,' I say.

'Who?'

'I don't know.'

Dr GRIFFITHS
Corrective
Surgery.

BEFORE

AFTER

She strides off and checks each of the aisles. Any moment now she's going to see Danny and throw him out. Good riddance I reckon.

'I can't see anybody,' she says. 'Perhaps you'd better tell me how these books really ended up on the floor.'

I don't know what to say.

Over Mrs Wharton's shoulder I can see the A–G fiction shelf rocking back and forth. Danny's gone crazy. The excitement of thinking he's invisible has gone to his head. I've got to stop him before he goes too far.

'Excuse me, Mrs Wharton,' I say. 'Back in a minute.'

'Where do you think you're going?'

I dash to the seriously rocking shelf to try to pull Danny away and bring him to his senses, but it's already too late. The shelf tilts too far to the right. All the books fall onto the carpet. The force of the bookshelf striking the next shelf pushes it over and the combined weight of these two pushes the third shelf over. Just like a row of dominoes. Except heavier. And louder.

There is silence. Nobody can believe what they've just seen.

Mrs Wharton is speechless. She is just standing there with her mouth open.

But Danny hasn't finished yet.

He's approaching Mrs Wharton from behind, one of her prized hanging-basket ferns in his hand. The ferns that she waters so lovingly every morning before school.

Danny's staring straight ahead and carrying the pot plant in his raised out-stretched arms, like its the AFL Premiership Cup.

'No!' I yell, but it's like he's posessed.

He tips it upside down over Mrs Wharton's head. Fern fronds and clumps of dirt and little white fertiliser pellets spill all over her hair, down her face and onto her dress. They collect in a pile at her feet.

GREAT PLACES TO HIDE.

Danny is just standing there laughing. Poor guy. He really thinks he's invisible.

Mrs Wharton wheels around.

'Just what do you think you're doing?' she says to him.

'Who?' he says.

'You!' she says, going red in the face.

'But you can't see me,' says Danny. 'I'm invisible!'

'Invisible? Well, we'll see about that!' she says.

WEIRD
PLACES
TO HIDE.

HUMAN
BODY
PARTS
Nº 47B.

The
Tongue

She reaches out, grabs his ear and twists it at least 360 degrees – and then – judging by the expression on Danny's face – another 360 degrees after that.

Danny drops to his knees in pain.

'Oww! Oww! Let go!' he says.

'There,' she says. 'Feeling a little more visible now?'

I must admit I'm rather enjoying the spectacle. After all, Danny had no qualms about getting me into trouble.

Mrs Wharton lets go of his ear.

'Now,' she says, looking from Danny to me, 'both of you pack up your books, and

Now you're being silly!

120

get straight to the principal's office! And consider yourselves banned from the library for the rest of the year.'

Both of us? The rest of the year? Great. There goes my history assignment. And my English wide reading. And my social studies research. How could Danny be so dumb?

I gather up my books. There's no use arguing.

Mrs Wharton escorts us to the door and slams it behind us.

'Danny,' I say, turning to face him, 'you are an idiot. Did you really think . . .'

But I don't finish my question. Danny's not there.

'Danny?' I say. 'Where are you?'

I hear a giggle and then a tremendous burp in my right ear. It's so loud it almost ruptures my ear-drum.

I spin around.

'Danny?'

But there's no sign of him – no visible sign anyway – just the sound of his crazy laughter echoing down the empty corridor.

Great Cat Ambushes.

cat's food

He He

Great HUMAN Ambushes.

The principal can wait. I'm going straight to sick bay.

I'm feeling a little faint myself.

A TerrIBLE christmas and a Sappy new year

Sunday afternoon.

Jen's Christmas cards are sitting on the table. All fifty thousand of them in three big stacks. The envelopes aren't sealed, so I figure that means she wants me to open them and have a look.

I open the top envelope. The card has a picture of a big jolly Santa's face on it.

The message on the inside reads: Dear Kerrie, wishing you a Merry Christmas and a Happy New Year, love Jen.

Very original . . . not!

The second card has exactly the same picture on it.

And inside Jen has written exactly the same greeting: Dear Sandra, wishing you a Merry Christmas and a Happy New Year, love Jen.

She has written the same thing on every card. The only bit that changes is the name of the person she's sending it to.

SANTA BOARS!

There's only one thing to do.

I grab some liquid paper, a black sharpie and set to work.

I don't have much time. Jen will be wanting to catch the six o'clock post.

On the first card I draw heavy dark eyebrows over Santa's twinkling eyes. He's not looking quite so jolly now.

But still, it's not enough. I draw a scar running from the corner of his right eye to the corner of his mouth. I black out one of his front teeth and give him a black eye. And just for fun I add a couple of Frankenstein bolts to each side of his neck. That's much better.

Now for the greeting on the inside. Merry Christmas? I don't think so. I change the M on *Merry* to a T, cross out the Y and add

IBLE to the end. And a happy new year? Not if I replace the H on *Happy* with S. Much nicer . . . A TerrIBLE Christmas and a Sappy New Year.

I go through the rest of the cards, changing the greetings and adding eyebrows, scars, moustaches, nose-rings, eyebrow-rings, tattoos, antennae and Martian ears to the Santas. By the time I've finished, no two Santas are alike. The only thing they have in common is that if you saw any of them coming towards you on the street, you'd turn and run the other way.

NEW SITE FOR THE BEST PRACTICAL JOKE EVER. Pg 70

I put each card carefully back into its envelope so it doesn't look like they've been messed with.

And – as if brightening up her Christmas cards isn't enough – I even take the trouble to find Jen and ask her if she'd like me to run them down to the postbox for her.

SLEEP PILLS

She asks me if I'm feeling all right.

I tell her that Christmas is a time for giving and that doing things for her makes me happy.

FiX Santa

What..?

She accuses me of sucking up because it's Christmas.

If only she knew . . .

The postbox is over the other side of the hill.

There are so many cards I almost get repetitive strain injury putting them in the box. But at last they're all posted.

I'm feeling pretty happy with myself.

Jen's friends all think they're so sophisticated. I can just imagine the looks on their faces when they see their mutant Santas. They'll think Jen has lost her mind. Maybe they'll kick her out of the gang for being so childish. That would be excellent. Then maybe she could get some new friends. Some nice ones.

And then an awful thought occurs to me. What if Jen's friends retaliate? What if they start sending cards back to her wishing *her* a terrible Christmas – or worse? I wouldn't put it past them.

It's not going to take Jen long to figure

out that I had something to do with it.

And then she'll punish me by giving me a horrible present – or even worse – no present at all.

Maybe this joke wasn't such a great idea after all . . .

I have to get those cards back out of the box!

Luckily, the postbox has a parcel handle. Being Christmas time, the box will probably be so full that Jen's cards will be right on top. Getting them back is going to be easy.

I pull the handle towards me and slide my arm into the parcel slot. Standing on the tips of my toes, I ease the handle away from me and try to curl my arm down into the box. But it doesn't work. My arm is jammed against the back of the parcel chute. My fingers are nowhere near the letters. There must be a better way.

I could get a fishing line with a hook on the end of it and try fishing them out. No, that would take too long.

It's getting late. I'm getting desperate.

DO YOU HAVE TO VISIT THE SCHOOL PRINCIPAL?

Charm him/her by sticking bananas up your nostrils. Works every time. TRUST US!

Perhaps I could build a fire around the bottom of the box so that it heats up and becomes like a huge oven and incinerates everything inside it.

Or maybe I could grab the hose from the house opposite and fill the box with water. Then the ink on the front of the envelopes would smudge and run and the post office won't know where to send them.

They are both brilliant plans, but neither would be fair to the innocent letters already in the box. I don't want to stop them getting through – I just want Jen's letters back.

I hear a squeal of brakes behind me.

I turn around. It's the postman!

'Am I glad to see you,' I say. 'I just posted some letters, but I think I forgot to put the postcodes on and I was wondering if you could get them back for me.'

'Sorry, mate,' says the postman, 'I can't help you. I'm not allowed to do that.'

He puts a sack underneath the door and turns the key.

Hundreds of letters flow into the sack.

'Besides, it'd take ages to find your letters

in amongst this lot,' he says. 'Go down to the post office. They might be able to help.'

'But I can't get there now,' I say. 'It's too late.'

He shrugs. 'Too bad.'

'Please?' I say. 'It's a matter of life and death.'

'So's my job,' says the postman. He gets into his van and zooms off.

So much for Christmas spirit.

AMAZING EYE TRICKS #5 * ANSWER.
At first sight it seems that circle 'b' is the bigger. But actually 'a' is bigger. It looks smaller because it's further away.

* see pg 137.

I don't see much of Jen for the rest of the week, until Friday afternoon. The mail arrives late. There's the usual boring letters for Mum and Dad, a couple of cards for Jen and, as usual, nothing for me.

I go to Jen's room and knock on her door.

'Yes?' she says.

'Some letters for you,' I say.

She opens the door. Her eyes are puffy, as if she's been crying. I hand her the envelopes. She takes them without a word and closes the door.

What to wear for work experience!

The Accountants.

A few minutes later I hear loud sobs coming from her room.

I can guess why. It's just as I feared. Her friends are retaliating by sending her horrible cards. I should confess, but how can I?

And what if Father Christmas finds out? He only comes to *good* boys and girls. What a dumb prank to play right before Christmas.

Due to lack of space, the <u>best</u> practical joke ever has been moved to Pg 24.

It's the night before Christmas. I'm in the lounge. It's dark, except for the blinking of the Christmas tree lights.

I've just put out a glass of milk and some chocolate-chip cookies for Santa, like I do every year. I've laid a pillowcase on a chair and written my name on it in black sharpie so he'll know it's mine. I'm just adding a few last-minute items to my letter to Santa when I hear the unmistakable sounds of jingling and reindeer hooves on the roof.

He's early!

I quickly fold the letter and stuff it into the envelope.

But before I can get out of the room, there is a huge crash. And then a stream of angry cursing. Well, I think it's cursing. Some of the words are new to me, but they sound like the sort of thing I'd get into trouble for repeating.

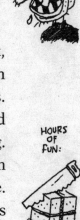

What to wear for work experience:
At the Dentists

A cloud of black soot explodes from the fireplace, followed by Santa.

At least, I think it's Santa . . .

There's no big white beard or red suit, and he's as skinny as a rake. He is clad in black leather with chains and silver studs. His face is covered in dark three-day-old stubble and one of his front teeth is missing. He has a black eye and a scar running from the corner of his mouth to his other eye. And, worst of all, little Frankenstein bolts coming out of his neck.

He seems strangely familiar. Where have I seen this man before?

And then I remember.

I created him. He's one of the mutant Santas from Jen's Christmas cards.

HOURS OF FUN:

Saw all your family's Xmas presents in half.

131

'Stop right there, you little weasel!' he booms. 'It's time all *good* children were in bed! What are you doing still up?'

'I-I-I was in bed,' I say, 'but then I remembered I'd forgotten to put out some cookies and a glass of milk for you.'

'Milk?' he snarls, and then spits into the fireplace. He picks up the glass and throws the milk in my face. 'Milk? Haven't you got anything stronger? It's cold out there, you know! And as for these . . . '

Santa picks up the chocolate-chip cookies in his bony hands and crumbles them into dust.

'These are for kids! I travel all the way from the North Pole and you think a few cookies will satisfy my hunger. I want a steak! Medium rare! Now!'

'I'll see what I can do,' I say. I run to the kitchen and open the freezer. There are no steaks. All we've got is veggie-burgers. Completely frozen. I guess they'll have to do. I grab the box and go back to the loungeroom.

'Well?' he says.

'Would you like a frozen veggie-burger?'

I say, offering the box.

He shakes his head.

'You're wasting my time,' he says. 'What's that in your other hand?'

I'm still holding my letter to Santa.

'It's a letter for you . . .' I say. 'With a few of the things I was hoping for . . .'

'Give it here!' he says, striding over and snatching it out of my hand.

But he doesn't read it. He wipes his nose with it, crumples it into a ball and throws it into the fireplace.

He sniffs loudly and reaches into a black duffle bag that's slung over his shoulder.

WEIGHT LOSS
CLINIC

"I feel looka
lighter and
10 years
younger"

'Okay, Mr Vege-loving-tarian! Since you like vegetables so much, this is for you. Catch!'

He throws me a small silver ball.

It stinks.

'Open it,' he says.

I peel off a bit of the foil. The smell gets worse.

'Keep going!'

I keep peeling the foil. It's a potato. Dark-grey. Mouldy. Stinking.

BOO!

POP!

133

'Now,' says Santa, 'eat it!'

And he laughs and he laughs and that's when I wake up – with a horrible taste in my mouth – wishing I'd never played that stupid childish practical joke on Jen.

Christmas is now only five days away. I've had the rotten potato dream the last three nights in a row. I'm too scared to sleep. I've got to tell Jen what I've done.

I can hear her talking in the kitchen. I get out of bed. I've got to confess.

I open the kitchen door. Jen is yelling. She sees me and slams the telephone down.

'What do you want, you little snoop?' she snaps. She's holding a card. There's a ripped envelope on the floor.

'Nothing,' I say and go straight out. She's obviously had another fight with one of her friends. She'll probably be friendless for the rest of her life.

And it's all my fault.

It's the night before Christmas. There's a large box wrapped in gold paper underneath the Christmas tree. I hadn't noticed it until now. My name's on the card. And it's from Jen! I hold it up to my ear and shake it. No clues. I peel a bit of the sticky tape away from one end of the paper to try to get a glimpse of what it is.

'Oh, hi,' says Jen. 'I see you've found your present.'

I jump in fright, drop the present and turn around.

'Yes, I mean, no, I wasn't doing anything,' I stutter.

'It's okay,' she says. 'It's your present. Merry Christmas.'

'Thanks, Jen.'

But instead of making me happy it makes me feel even *more* guilty.

I betrayed her trust.

I defaced her cards.

All her friends hate her – and it's all my fault.

It's now or never.

'Um – Jen – this is probably a really great present and all, but I really don't deserve it . . . you see, I changed your cards . . . and I've been feeling really bad about it . . .'

CORPORATE
SANTA

'So it *was* you!' she says. 'I thought so!'

'I know it was wrong,' I say. 'But . . .'

'Wrong? No, it was brilliant!'

'Huh?' I say, so surprised I almost fall over. 'But over the last couple of weeks you've seemed really upset – I thought it was my fault.'

'Oh that,' she laughs. 'I broke up with Rob, but it's no big deal. We made up last night.'

'So, you actually liked the cards?'

'My friends loved them!' she says. 'You've started a real craze. Come and see!'

She takes me to her bedroom.

This is a very special privilege. She once told me that if I ever came in here she would personally pull out each and every one of my teeth with a rusty pair of pliers – without anaesthetic.

She points to an enormous bunch of cards on her window sill.

I can't believe my eyes.

On each of the cards there is a different sort of Santa. A sneering punk Santa with a safety pin through his nose. A long-haired heavy metal Santa playing a guitar solo on his reindeer's antlers. There're grunge Santas, hip-hop Santas, hippy Santas, Frankenstein Santas – even a dreadlocked Reggae Santa smoking a huge white cigar. Wow! Who would've ever thought Jen's friends had a sense of humour?

'Just promise me one thing,' says Jen. 'Don't tell anybody you changed the cards. See, they all think it was my idea and I'd kind of like to keep it that way.'

'Okay,' I say, 'as long as you promise me something.'

'What's that?'

'Don't breathe a word about this to Santa.'

Jen puts a finger up to her mouth. 'My lips are sealed,' she says.

If you would like more AMAZING EYE TRICKS write to "AMAZING EYE TRICKS" P.O. BOX EM3W ●L B●

HO HO

TOYS

SANTASTEIN'S MONSTER.

I was a Xmas Bon-Bon and I didn't even get a PARTY HAT... or a whistle!! That's it!! I've had enough!!! THIS IS THE END!!!

137

END

COMING SOON
FROM THE INTERNATIONALLY
BESTSELLING CREATORS OF
THE TREEHOUSE SERIES

 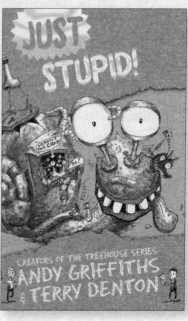

Just Annoying! and *Just Stupid!* are the
next two books in Andy and Terry's hilarious series
about the world's smartest, craziest and most
annoying practical joker!